HALFWAY UP THE MOUNTAIN

By

Kiran Khalap

MARION BOYARS
LONDON · NEW YORK

Published in Great Britain and the United States in 2005 by
MARION BOYARS PUBLISHERS LTD
24 Lacy Road, London, SW15 1NL

First published in India in 2003 by Jacaranda Press

www.mar

Distributed i
Kuring-gai, N

Printed in 20
10 9 8 7 6 5

Copyright

All rights re

No part of
transmitted
recording c
prior writt

The right of Kiran Khalap to be identified as author of this work has been asserted
by him in accordance with the Copyright, Designs and Patents Act 1988.

A CIP catalogue record for this book is available from the British Library.
A CIP catalog record for this book is available from the Library of Congress.

ARTS COUNCIL ENGLAND The publishers would like to thank the Arts Council of England for
assistance with the marketing of this book.

ISBN 0-7145-3113-8
13 digit ISBN 978-0-7145-3113-7

Printed in England by Bookmarque, London

To my father, Vishnudas Bhaskar Khalap,
who fought many fierce battles against mediocrity, and
won quite a few.

Mediocre:
adj 1. Of middling quality, neither good nor bad.
2. Second rate {Latin *medius* (middle) + *ochris* (rugged mountain)}

❧ 1 ❧
A Taste of Death

THE FINAL DAY in June is unusually quiet. The village air is skittish with ions. Cows rush about on stubble-covered fields, tails stiff, hind legs kicking air. Pot-bellied clouds come unstuck from the sky. They float down helplessly incontinent, leaking static. Your father attempts to 'shoo' the moment away by chanting louder his daily diet of *shlokas*. Your mother avoids looking at him. Two reluctant culprits wait for an unknown signal.

Some million volts of electricity break the standoff. They race down a kilometre from the clouds, rip up air molecules in their path, and announce the beginning of sorrow in your life with a thundersnap.

It's time.

Your father plucks you off the wooden swing in the porch and hugs you until you are unable to breathe. Then he lays you back gently on the huge teak seat, turns and rushes down the steps of the house.

You've always been an undemanding child, but somehow you sense the finality of the event. You jump off the swing, rush after him. Behind you, the teak seat is a lonely wail of a pendulum.

Your scream precedes you.

'*Baabaa*!'

He freezes. He should have left at night, while you were sleeping, as his guru had advised him last week. He should have.

It rains straight. Silver threads bind earth to sky. It rains so neither father nor daughter needs to hide the tears.

Your father has gritted himself for the blow of this moment. But you stand defenceless.

Their scaly backs glistening, black hoods trembling in tension, snakes of a hundred questions appear in your mind.

It rains in your mind.

The two of you stand in the courtyard separated by a common bond of yearning while your mother corks her sobs with her *pallu* rolled into a ball, tasting the metallic *zari* thread, partner in crime, yet not. Your brothers, older than you by many years, stand silent. *Bhai* is silent because he knows something. *Dada*, almost deaf and dumb, is silent because he doesn't know anything.

You can't look up at your father's face, dare not. So you stare at his huge fist, flesh coarsened by plough and brass bells, and, as a man with tobacco breath will whisper urgently in your ears a few decades later, the blood of a child your age. You just reach for his little finger, and clutch it in your terrified fist.

Your drum-taut tummy struggles against your skirt, as you break into sobs.

He kneels in the slush, holds your arms, and cries in a hoarse voice, 'Promise me, you will not forget what I taught you...you will always be happy...like a goddess...*chidanandarupah*...even without me, without anybody...promise me?'

You nod, clutch harder, not knowing what he wants, what it implies. Four decades will pass before you understand your own promise. Anything, something, to keep him with you for a little while more. He hugs you, then unwraps your arms from around his neck, kisses your forehead and stands up.

The rain stops. Your father turns and marches off. A peacock's cry cuts the moment into two clean halves. The wooden swing screeches to a halt.

For an eternity, your sense of the self vanishes. You are the sound of a sparrow drying itself, you are the wetness of the rain in your hair, you are the green leaves lit by grey half-light, but there is no centre, no you. You don't understand what is happening to you, but you don't want this state to end.

The first sensation that breaks the luminous nothingness is a shadow. It is *Dada*. He holds your shoulders and shakes you. You stare at the ground, at your tiny feet with the squishy mud between your toes, refusing to budge. *Dada* lifts you up in a fireman's lift, carries you into the house, where your mother is curled up in a corner.

For days, the house remains under a bell jar of silence.

Maya.

Illusion.

The word's genealogy leads us to the Sanskrit word '*mri*', meaning 'measurement'. When the mind measures, it distances itself from reality.

The beginning of measurement is the beginning of illusion.

Somebody should have warned your father: if you name your daughter Illusion, you can't keep hold of her for too long.

Dada uses every trick in his book to make you smile. He knots the coarse tresses of the ficus in the backyard into a swing very different from the one in the porch. Every time you sit on it and he pushes you, the sky *swooshes* closer, yet you refuse to scar it with your usual shrieks of delight. He creates a funny dumbbell by placing circular cowdung cakes at two ends of a stick, paints moustaches on himself like the village wrestlers have, and feigns pain as he picks the dumbbell off the ground.

Your lips smile, your eyes don't.

One late afternoon in the monsoon *Dada* attempts to create river magic for you. He drags you to its edge, while the clouds unload their moist bundles. *Dada* clucks his tongue at his favourite buffalo, Shankar, places you on his back, then sits behind you, hanging on to the gigantic cusp of horns. When *Dada* clucks again, Shankar leaps into the roiling waters. The water has a life of its own; it splashes on your face, makes you gasp. You remember the smell of fear and *Dada*'s skin and the roughness of the buffalo's hide, but *Dada* has done this before and you trust him more than anybody else. You clutch him hard, and when you return to the safety of the bank, a heroic act achieved but not announced to the rest of the world, somehow you both know it is futile.

Your father has fractured the neck of your childhood.

Only school hours remain untouched. Sitting on the cotton carpet, reciting your quarter, half and three-quarter tables without understanding what the words mean, you watch a square sky.

A kite tears into the edge of one cloud, then lazes up vertically, carrying taut the thread of its flight, and swiftly stitches in the second cloud's edge. The threesome drifts out of the frame of the window, leaving the slate of your mind squeaky clean once again.

'Where does the wind blow from at night, sea or land? How many hours in a day, how many minutes in an hour? What was the Rani of Jhansi's real name?' The answers pop in your head even as the teacher asks the questions. So the teacher avoids asking you till the rest of the class has failed. She wonders how you remember so much, but never speak.

Maya, the silent one.

Bhai, your eldest brother, looks after the family gods now. On your long walk home, while you collect a bunch of white *paarijaat* flowers with orange stalks to make 'holy water' for *Bhai*, *Dada* stands guard, shooing away the cows that are going to the river to slake their thirst. You put the flowers in a bag created by lifting your long skirt, loudly chanting the *shloka* taught to you.

'*Manobuddhi ahankaar chittaani naaham, na cha shrotrajivhe...*'

'I am not mind, or intellect, ego or consciousness. I am neither hearing nor speech. I am pure bliss...'

The chant means as little to you as the half tables, though you like the shiny copper texture of this sound more than the black and white marble texture of the tables. Without your knowledge, the chant will become tattooed on the skin of your consciousness. Its meaning will guide you along the labyrinths of fate.

Green-eyed priest Chintamani, senior Brahmin, who is walking back home for lunch after having bathed, clothed and anointed the ever-awake goddess of village Wada, is not very sure he likes your chants. He walks past, muttering his own *shlokas*; decides to complain to the other elders in the village that you should not be permitted to dance with ghosts and gods alike.

Your tired mother follows the diktats of the age and co-opts you in her daily womanly grind. Girls need not be educated too much: after all, you don't need to know quadratic equations to raise children.

Little does she know what the womb of your future holds. It is precisely your inability to give birth to children on schedule that will add a sting to the tail of your fate.

So you spend more time with her than at school. You are an equally quick apprentice in front of the smoky fire. Even your dour *Bhai* admits that you cook as well as your mother does. You learn to make perfectly circular *chapatis* with their four-skinned tummies puffed up by air.

You learn the difficult festive cooking: steamed translucent pancakes with the turmeric leaf fragrance, *puran polis* with blotting-paper-dry surface ready to suck up the coconut milk, *besan laddoos* that sit in glass containers with their floppy bellies distended by their own weight, and *modaks*, fluted edges hiding a delicious stuffing of coconut and jaggery.

The shape of the *modaks* will one day excite an elderly poet into comparing them to women's breasts, and whether you like it or not, you will receive rude, unsolicited stares in response to this analogy.

Drawing water from the well is something you enjoy, because you like the sequence of sounds. When the bucket rushes down and slaps the water's surface, the sound gathers body in the tunnel of the well. This rising column keeps getting scratched by the falling squeaks of the wheel, and then suddenly, in silence, out of the womb of the earth, sweet water mirroring the sky. You make the cotton wicks with unconscious ease, but even as the years pass by, lighting the lamps with those wicks sometimes wakes up questions.

In the room of the gods lies a treasure nobody has the key to, except you, because your father has taught you to read a new language. There are second-hand magazines, books, newspapers, a pocket dictionary, all in English.

Without a teacher, your father had strung meaning out of phrases, opened for himself the gates to unknown worlds. Worlds more dangerous to the Brahmins than the Brahmins had imagined. *Dada* watches you wide-eyed as you do the same.

You gobble up old *National Geographics*, *Look and Learn*, a theosophy book, *A Guide to Flora and Fauna in Western India*. Some phrases grow transparent over time, some don't. Sometimes you just stare at the illustrations; because the idioms are adamant, refusing to share their meaning.

However, the reading provides unusual perspectives, changing the world around you permanently. You visit nations where girls your age dress differently, you fly with comic strip heroes on machines vomiting flames, inside you sprout flowers that eat insects.

Your mother is worried you have given up the company of other girls. She forces you to attend the *mangalagaur* festival celebrations. It is an occasion mainly for young married girls who have returned to their mothers during the monsoons. It's the time for them to share their secrets with unmarried girls, dance a hundred whirling, squatting, jumping, energetic dances and sing quiz songs till the wee hours of the morning. While the red earth turns green and the air grows cooler, you rediscover the childhood abandon that your wiry body allows you, but somehow the rains always remind you of separation rather than union.

You slip out of the group, walk home alone.

One evening, as your mother and you sit rolling wicks for the permanently smiling gods, she unwraps a secret, avoiding your eyes.

She starts whispering about your father. She is the only one he had confided in, and you are now old enough to share her burden. She tells you about his interest in Western science and in *Aghora*, the Left Hand Path to Illumination.

'It started after *Dada*'s birth...he was shocked by his handicap.'

Apparently, your father could not figure out *Dada*'s congenital defect. In response, he had withdrawn from everything and everyone. He decided that he would unravel the mystery of the entire universe, the warp and weft of the *panchmahabhutaas*, the five great elements. He would travel outwards along the path of science and inwards along the path of mysticism.

He was a strong-willed man, able to stand alone, able to accept challenges that most men avoided. As an adolescent he had been the first to swim across the river in full spate. The first to refuse to be afraid of the wild boars on the hill. When they started destroying the farms, he led a team of youngsters against them, flushing them out with noisy drums and fire.

'How to tell you, Maya, how scared I was when he came to finalise our marriage proposal... I remember peering at him from behind my mother's *pallu*, as he sat alone, without any elders or relatives accompanying him. He sat looking straight at my father and spoke in that gravelly voice of his, "You don't need to give me a dowry because you are not buying a husband for your daughter...our marriage is not a transaction." Nobody did that kind of thing in our times. I wondered if he was that strict as a husband...but instead he treated me like an equal...always asking my permission before he did anything out of the ordinary.'

The village feared him because he feared nothing.

She talks about the rumours that he had committed human sacrifices, '...while all he did was yearn to sacrifice his own fear in the *smashaan*, the cremation ground, see?'

She talks about his new devotion: the goddess who ruled the Left Hand Path and her three aspects. *Ma*, the mother aspect, *Shakti*, the power aspect, and *Maya*, the delusive aspect.

After a long silence, still reluctant to relive the pain in the memories, you pick a scab off the cowdung floor, look up, and ask, 'So why did he name me after the goddess?'

'Because he believed you were born as proof of her love for him. Before that, only your brothers...so much older...and suddenly you...so fair, with deep eyes...see? He thought I was touched by the goddess, that...that she had entered my womb.'

Your voice is heavy with confusion. 'Then why did he leave us...leave his...goddess?'

'Because the *Aghori* guru who had introduced him to

the path came back after twelve years. The guru reminded him that if he wanted to become one with the goddess he had to give up his deepest attachment...and you had become his deepest attachment...you were the only one he cared for any longer...not *Bhai*, not *Dada*, not even me...see?'

You ask the next question from the edge of an abyss. 'So he left us...because of...me?'

In the darkness, in reply, your mother's calloused hand touches your face, shaking as she smothers an old sob. '*Shhh*...don't say that...don't. Nobody can decide who leaves why and when!'

The conversation has led to a trapdoor that creaks open by itself. You can no longer hold it shut. You are too young to fight the temptation. You tiptoe down a ladder, enter a dungeon of memories, walk towards your father and the other man you love as much.

ಌ 2 ಌ
Memories of Paradise

ONE: IT'S 1943, and you are a happy seven-year-old. You lie in the warm hammock of your father's lap, wearing a peacock green *parkar polka*, petticoat and blouse, shot with blue and crimson capillaries. He sits there with an ache instead of a heart, the ache of loving too much. He isn't aware that those blue and crimson capillaries will be the vehicles of his memories in your heart.

He is singing his favourite poems from 'Songs of the Madder Soil', a collection of verse that celebrates Konkan, this strip of land retrieved from the sea by a sage. His voice comes to you through his belly as you lie in his lap, and through the air as well.

The fireflies circle around the rising thermals of his voice, blinking in the warmth.

> '*When the steel fang bites,*
> *flesh will ooze*
> *madder blood now unfaithful,*
> *now unknown,*
> *till the palaces of our memory*

turn white, erect
propped by bone.

Our love for the buried umbilical
will not set us free
Our love for the munja gods
will not turn to stone
till the palaces of our memory
turn white, erect
propped by bone.'

The poet paladin, Krishna Khare, is young and beleaguered in a cruel mill city; he's pining for his birthplace. He migrated from gentle Konkan and discovered a heartless city. His swaying-palm rhythms stay with you. You will not believe it now, but on a rainy day that washes memories off the pages inside you, you will meet him.

Two: 1947. It's midnight, a year before your father will attempt to incinerate his own delusion, his own *maya*, by joining his *Aghori* guru's pilgrimage into darkness. Roughly two thousand kilometres from where you are, an erudite Prime Minister announces that a nation is born, fulfilling its tryst with destiny at the stroke of the hour. You are now a citizen of a free country, instead of a colony, yet you personally are destined to discover freedom through that hand-me-down language.

The silk of the darkness outside your window rustles. You get up and peer from under sleep-heavy eyelids. Your mother snores behind you, her sari smelling of sweat and asafoetida and turmeric and coconut oil, dog tired, after the eighteen-hour grind needed to feed a family of five three fresh meals a day.

You stare at a flickering obsidian face, its fangs bared. Luciferin and luciferase clash, ignite, emit cold mint-green light. A cicada's chirr shaves off one moment, shaves off two, shaves off three. Your cry of terror changes into a giggle as you recognise the face behind the smile. *Dada* smiles in return. His experiment with the fireflies stuffed inside the papaya peduncle and opening covered by muslin to create a home-made torch has been wildly successful.

You reach out and touch his face through the vertical iron bars, smell the coconut oil soot. The village girls use the soot to make kohl, and your father uses it to blacken a mirror so he can stare at it and forge an arrow out of his occult powers, to predict what awaits human beings in the darkness that surrounds the future.

If you had asked him then, he would have predicted the finality behind touching *Dada*'s face through iron bars. He might also have warned you about the recurrence of vertical bars as a motif in your life.

Three: in your dreams, you feed your nine-year-old senses on a feast of miracles. The water running through the channels for the banana plantation behind the red-tiled family house wears the skin of the sun. You splash a few drops onto the arum, watching them sparkle on the velveteen elephant-ears.

You press your ear to the xylem of the banana plants, as it noisily sucks up the moisture, irrigating the dry cell walls, nourishing tissue.

Years later, a poet will compare your inner thigh to the smooth white pillar of pith in a banana plant.

Four: '*Maaayaaa*!!!'

Your mother's call zigzags wingless over the viridian

shadows of betel nut palms, loses height, falls silent in your footprints.

'*Maaayaaa*!!!'

You are with *Dada*, running to get out of range of your mother's next call. You run barefoot with him, reaching the edge of the village river, gasping from excitement and effort. Uneasy in his twilight world of fuzzy sound, *Dada* has worked out a comforting equation: He will protect and entertain this doll of a sister, and in return, he'll be fed morsels of affection and admiration. You call him *Dada*; he calls you with an excited croak or with his dancing eyes.

The river is your favourite playground. There are sheets of sunshine put out to dry on the water here and there, but *Dada* isn't going to worry about laundry now. He climbs a bamboo on the bank, certain that you are watching wide-eyed. When he reaches the top, the spine of the bamboo arcs under his weight, squeaking as it lowers him into the black mirror of the surface, splashing a white bloom in his wake. His croak of delight drowns with him.

You lie on grass so tender the shadow of a flying egret crushes it. Above you are translucent hearts of jade, the sun alighting on *peepal* leaves.

'Want to hear the naiads?' he gestures, standing over you, blocking the jade, dripping rain on your eyes. You trust him enough to get up, walk into the water and flop down. The summer river snores, hibernating in interconnected pools, some shallow enough to display their gravelly insides, some deep enough to hide water ghosts and snakes with two heads.

'Close your eyes, hold your nose and put your head underwater,' he mimes his instructions, his round face distorting to communicate. You hear no naiads singing, but a huge bellow aspirates inside your frail chest. You hear the air rubbing against the cartilage of your windpipe, sandpapering it into smoothness. You hear your breath, your body's umbilical cord of oxygen, binding you to the universe.

That is when, for the first time, you taste infinity. You are lost in that sound and the darkness and in the tiny bubbles that tickle your back as they snake up from within your skirt. A scared *Dada* drags you out, stares at you questioningly. You grin, wipe the water out of your eyes with two podgy palms. You will revisit this moment and this river, but you'll be stark naked and seventeen years away.

As he leads you to the tree beside the temple, he cautions you with a finger on his lips and smiles. He carefully shoves his wet head into the dark hole of the ficus. Your hormones drum up an alliterative rhythm, fright flight fight fright flight fight fright flight fight, while *Dada*'s headless body stands motionless. Then a buzzing black ball emerges, attached to two spindly stems.

You gasp. '*Daadaa*!'

The bees of the River Goddess! They have completely covered *Dada*'s head! His eyes are closed against the tickling of their feet, so initially he turns away from you, then corrects his bearings and smiles.

Five: it is another night, when your father, dabbler in the occult and the scientific in equal measure, explains the mechanism of collective consciousness, of pheromones and terpenoids, the language of antennae brushing antennae.

You fall asleep in his lap, your thin limbs limp from too much excitement.

❦ 3 ❦

Destiny's Second Knot

YOUR ENTRY INTO WOMANHOOD is quiet. Your mother whispers to the brothers that the crow has touched you, that you need to sit separately for three days, in a corner between the bathroom and the kitchen. The corner is darkened by the smoke of the fire that heats the bath water, its wall heavy with the smell of ash, copper and steam. You get used to the simultaneous roughness and wetness of cloth between your thighs.

By some unknown signal, *Dada* understands that he can no longer come and hug you from behind, or lie with his head in your lap, watching you sing 'Songs of a Madder Soil'.

One sense out of many pulls its shutters down. Your body will wait patiently for a few years before it reopens those sluice gates.

Your father's departure has dismantled the fence of fear that protected your family. Priest Chintamani's glance leaves strands of saliva on your breasts, his attempts to bury them in the humus in his mind fail.

In his sleep, he touches soft fair flesh. His crotch

becomes a muslin tent.

Your mother now forces you to wear a sari. The one you wear when the boy comes down from Bombay to 'see you' is bright yellow. It is 1956, less than a decade since the first man in your life left without a forwarding address. Now you have to tie your fate to another, a stranger.

You peek at your husband-to-be while he slurps tea from a saucer smelling of Lifebuoy soap. Pockmarked face, sharp nose, thin body, thick curly hair. 'Ravindra', your elder brother whispers his name to you. Your father-in-law, Shantaram Patil a.k.a. *Nana*, in Terycot trousers and nylon shirt, with big gold ring warmed by the *beedi* held upright between the last two fingers, mixing tobacco smoke and air for a better kick, snaps his fingers to encourage the ash to submit to gravity, and mother-in-law, *Mai*, in a nine-yard sari, splayed toes with toe-rings and high-pitched voice, encourage him to ask questions of you.

'Like to live in Bombay?' Ravindra asks, not interested in your reply. You nod. *Bhai* brings them three dry-palm fans with cloth trimming. Father and son enjoy the novelty of the huge swing in your porch, cold iron hook screeches on iron loop, while in the half-light of the kitchen your mother and you sweat over the woodfire.

The wedding is heralded at dawn by the ruthless whips of cane on skin. The drumming wakes up green-eyed priest Chintamani, his subconscious heavy with the knowledge that he'll never again dare to dream of biting your nipples. You belong to another man.

By now, suspending your reactions has become a habit for you. You halt every emotion in mid-swing.

You are made to play wedding games. First, Ravindra,

your husband, and you, search for a coin submerged in a plate of turmeric water; a game invented to enable two strangers to touch fingertips and exchange electricity.

The second game shakes you out of the exile of your senses: a sliver of coconut flesh has to be nibbled at from both sides by bride and bridegroom. His moustache tickles your lips, you cannot help bursting into laughter.

An ancient culture, despite being colonised, has remembered well its job of gently stoking the fire of the skin.

You remember your ungainly mother, sniffling, whispering, as she makes you wear her only pair of gold bangles. Two bands of solidified sunshine, her last legitimate possession, your last female-to-female bond, now shine around your wrist. The previous night she had smiled, 'See, I had promised him, your father, that whatever happens, I will make sure you enter a good home. See, it is happening. If he were here, he would have cried more than when he abandoned you...you were the centre of his life. But don't worry, I will be here, always, for you, that was my promise to him.'

Unfortunately, human promises have a habit of being subject to the laws of nature. Neither of you are aware that the next time you see her, your mother will be trussed up like an ungainly reindeer.

Your husband has already confirmed his bond with you by tying a necklace around your fair neck. A necklace of black beads ending in four tiny cups of gold that clasp your breastbone. A four-chambered stethoscope listening to your four-chambered heart.

Your *mangalsutra*, the auspicious thread of belonging.

'I am yours, for better or for worse.'

You touch your mother's and *Bhai*'s feet when you leave home. *Dada* carries your dowry trunk in his right hand and clutches your right hand with his left. The trunk contains your mother's gift of bangles, a few saris that came as wedding presents from relatives, some books, and deep down, hidden by it all, the tiny *parkar polka* that you had worn when your father departed. Green shot with blue and crimson capillaries. Your secret tapestry of pain.

You remember your *Dada* clutching the bars of the State Transport bus window till his knuckles turned white, his eyes pleading for an answer, 'Why must you go, why must you go, why must you go?'

All you can do is push your hand through the iron bars, horizontal this time, and cup his face.

'Why? I don't know. I am the last person to understand why anybody leaves.'

❧ 4 ❧

Among the Ecological Refugees

THE CITY OF BOMBAY demands its own sacrifices. It demands that your eyes must forget the horizon and the sunrise, your nose must forget cowdung and *nirmaalya*, the smell of stale flowers and milk and water offered to gods, your skin must forget the knotted skin of the ficus.

Your new home is a hundred and fifty square feet dovecote, and the only light is from the front, where it faces a narrow lane. You enter your home after toppling a rice bowl with your foot over the threshold; you will exit far less ceremoniously.

Three hundred human beings are crowded in the creaking structure of Maska Chawl, unspooling their destinies in humid boxes. Every family knows every other family, so the only private spaces are inside your head. Yet each lives so close to the edge of financial abyss, each will offer time and an affectionate hand on the back, but never money.

Instead of bathing in the dark copper-fragrant bathroom inside the kitchen in your village home, you bathe behind a flimsy curtain in the corner of the room.

Your body is never exposed to your own eyes. Instead of relieving yourself in the open air at dawn before too many men have woken up in the village, you shut yourself in a stinking tiny toilet used by tens of other human beings. The world closes in on you, tightening space so you are left with just enough to breathe.

Your parents-in-law like your silence, mistake it for docility. *Nana*'s lungs are spongy bags filled with fluff, a result of having lived in the mill for nights without end. His eyes are weak, designed to inhabit pelagic murkiness. *Mai* is glad you are there to lend her a hand. It's a fried-coconut-paste-based cooking test, a pickle and *papad*-making test, a wicks-for-the-ancient-gods-in-the-tiny-wooden-cabinet-above-the-bed-making test.

You pass with flying colours.

You are curious to see where *Nana* works. You have heard of a cloth mill from your father, you've dreamt of it through the urban poet, Krishna Khare's eyes, but you want to see it for yourself.

> *'Men go in,*
> *shells come out,*
> *their laughter will be hollow*
> *and so will our own*
> *till the palaces of our memory*
> *turn white, erect*
> *propped by bone.'*

Nana laughs it off. Young women do not visit mills. However, when you ask a third time, he indulges you, his brand new daughter-in-law, future carrier of his family name. He insists on Ravindra accompanying you.

The mill is a stone zoo populated by prehistoric iron monsters, saw-toothed, rustskinned, roundheaded, their jugulars bursting tight with grease and oil. It swallows brown men and white cotton and belches smoke in contented black puffs.

Nana's colleagues suppress their whistles and comments when he explains who you are, but he cannot help smiling at a couple of comments on the colour of your skin.

The noise knocks your breath off, yet you blush as you hear fragments of jokes about donkey penises making holes in *medu vadas* and the watermelon tits of Hindi film stars. It's a blunt world, a world where men spill the acid of their wit on the tedium of their jobs. You do not want to return.

Mai experiences her greatest glory when she discovers your ability to read and write English. One late afternoon the postman brings a letter to the door. You look at it and tell the postman that it's actually addressed to one of your neighbours, the Dhotres, Room 43 under the staircase. Their only son has been asked to present himself for an interview at a 'foreign' bank within seventy-two hours.

In the evening, Sanjay, the Dhotres' son, comes to thank you. Imagine if the letter had remained with your Marathi-speaking household by mistake. His entire family's future would have been different. Soon, Maska Chawl has developed the collective awareness that Patil the sign-painter's bride can read and write English. Sandhya, Sanjay's sister and the only girl in the chawl to use nail polish and carry a scented handkerchief to the common toilet, asks you if she can take lessons whenever you are free. She works at a factory that weaves gods out of coloured beads, pasting them on dark blue or crimson velvet. English can help her rise from worker to supervisor.

You smile in agreement, happy to have connected with someone who is not related by birth. In the village, the relationships were governed so much by their defined roles, you would have to think hard before you remembered *Bhai* or *Dada*'s real names.

That Saturday, the parents-in-law announce their plan to see the 'last show' of the new movie at Jai Mata cinema hall. Apparently, *Nana* is to retire that Monday, and what better way to celebrate than to overdo his second addiction? He will celebrate his departure from a dark, prehistoric mill world by visiting another dark, two-dimensional illusion. He has watched quite a few movies along with his only son, and there are times when both have hummed the same ditty, leaving you and *Mai* staring back uncomprehendingly.

Only later you realise the visit has been timed so you and Ravindra can, as a lawyer might put it, consummate your marriage.

Mai smells of naphthalene balls because she's wearing her wedding sari extracted out of the green trunk that holds the valuables of the family. All the tiny dreams and leaps of the heart crystallised into soft and hard objects, silk and metal, a four-colour paper god, a stone with a glissading name '*shaligraam*', the 'l' a retroflex so inverted that unless you've practised Sanskrit your tongue will knot itself into a cow hitch.

Nana, who is in a festive mood, slaps *Mai*'s bottom, winks at Ravindra, and sings a song that you don't catch, but sends Ravindra into uncontrollable giggles.

Mai shows mock anger at this churlishness, clearly enjoying the attention of both males in the family. They draw the door shut behind them, which rarely happens in Maska Chawl.

You two must be the most awkward first-timers on earth.

Outside, rats nibble at moonbeams. The white powder drifts to the soil, covering it with satin sparks, unable to prevent the ammonia vapours that rise from tens of drunken men's piss. The mill's Time Office manager lurches past, singing to the crumbling moon, just in time to smother your cry of pain. You anoint Ravindra's stump of lust with fluids that smell of the sea and fish from the Konkan.

As someone who spent so much time with herself, you believed you knew every millimetre of your body, but it has sprung a surprise. In damp recesses, under hidden lips, it had stored secret receptors. They tap out a code to spark off sheet lightning under your skin.

As if emboldened by this gawky union, Ravindra reaches into the trunk that held *Mai*'s secrets for so long, and pulls out a roll of art paper. He smoothes out the sheets, and in the jaundiced light of the 40W bulb, reveals his heart.

'I hope you don't laugh, I hope you don't smirk, you speak English and I don't, I hope you don't laugh, my brand new wife.'

You gaze at his drawings in silence. Genuine cartridge paper, 6B pencil, not one eraser mark. You stare at his pockmarked face, at the moustache. 'My husband. Maybe he is not a sign-painter, maybe he is an artist, like the one in the *National Geographic*'s article on Paris.' Something from the past survived, muscled up the brain, guided invisibly your husband's fingers (steady now!) till he recreated a world all his own.

'Why didn't you become an artist?'

He replies with a question, 'Is it good?'

You place your hand on his.

'It's different, it's not about the mill or the grime or the life around you, it's not trivial.'

'Is it good, Maya?' Contrary to tradition, he hasn't changed your given name after marriage.

'If I had had this talent...'

Your confession is cut short by the knock on the door.

Your parents-in-law are puzzled by the open trunk, but *Mai* is too tired to ask, and *Nana*'s drunken smile says he has started post-retirement celebrations in grand style.

When *Mai* and *Nana* sleep in the afternoon, you write long letters to *Dada* and your mother. They are letters meant to reassure your mother that the in-laws are happy about her training: her catering training, her worship training, her daughter-in-law training.

It's your elder brother *Bhai* who will read the letters out aloud to your illiterate mother, while *Dada* will stare at them, dreaming of the sunshine in your smile.

Almost a year after your marriage, Ravindra and you go to Matheran, the hill resort closest to Bombay. Ravindra can afford this trip since his employer, Goverdhan*Bhai* Patel has paid him more than he expected for his new signboards.

For you, it's like opening the doors of a locked house. Light and smells stream in, say, 'Hello, we're back, Maya, your childhood friends.' The humid blanket of Bombay air is replaced by a thin purity that you can taste in your throat. Ravindra doesn't realise it, but you've never been in a train before. In a burst of spontaneity, he climbs off the train as it inches along the mountainside, lopes along, leaps back in. Your scream is leavened half-sugary by delight, half-acrid by fear.

It's a conference of surprises. Ravindra's grey exterior sloughs off, you discover him wearing a crisp smile. He mimics a million characters in Maska Chawl, making you laugh at the spontaneity and accuracy of the portrayals. He insists that both of you ride horses since it is the best way of negotiating the soft earth trails in Matheran. Then, just when you have coped with the awkward up and down of the horse's gait, he slaps the rump of the horse you are riding. It gallops ahead startled, and you clutch the reins in terror, while the horse owner runs after you two. You feign anger when Ravindra catches up with you, but you can't suppress a grin when he imitates your expressions and your scream.

At Echo Point, he discovers your voice. You recite 'Songs of the Madder Soil'. He notes the peculiar colours and shape of your voice, cerulean blue made pregnant by a string of teardrops.

> *'Tell me my heart*
> *when the stained millcloth*
> *reveals more than it can hide*
> *Tell me what to do*
> *when every sunset deepens*
> *the wound in my side.*
>
> *Tell me what happened*
> *why sinew sells like hide*

Tell me what to do
when every sunset deepens
the wound in my side.

Hungry soot swallows light
Till there are no pupils in eyes
No sunrise will now cure
The wound in my side.'

You tell him what your father believed, how writing and painting and singing send spores of your self floating out, indestructible spores that bloom the moment they dock into other people's minds anywhere, somewhere, creating a web of shared understanding.

He tells you about his childhood. How he was rarely good at anything in school except drawing, and how his schoolmates did him favours at exams in exchange for his science and geography diagrams. Until he met you and showed you his sketches, nobody had said he was out of the ordinary.

The two of you stare across the valley, soaked in each other's memories. You hold him because you want to protect his fragile gift, he holds you because you were the first to acknowledge it.

The dusk-smeared mountains have tucked up their skirts after a hot day, to air their quilted cellulite.

He shouts out across the valley, 'What is it that the rich store in their pockets, while the poor throw away?'

Since the mountainside is nonplussed, he turns to you. You shake your head, 'I don't know either'. Eyes twinkling, he blows his nose. A green moth flies across the sun's rays, answering his question. The rich blow their noses in their handkerchiefs and keep them in their pocket, while the poor don't!

Ravindra opens up even more when the rest of the world recedes. He puts his arm around your back, protecting you from the ice cold shower of stars. 'Maya, I'll become an artist, get a job in a company?' You hold his turpentine-stained palm in yours and kiss it. It's a gesture you have borrowed from an Anaïs Nin heroine.

In a country that forgot its heritage of the art of love, books are your only access to the arcane dialect between men and women.

'I hope you get a job, but you must do more than just get a job, you must show us how to see differently, you know, lead us where your imagination leads you, away from anything that binds you,' you tell him.

He lays his head in your lap, mimicking the mushy Hindi film heroes as he asks with a smile, 'Not away from you, Mrs Patil, eh?'

You have been running your fingers through his hair. You stop. The cold of the stone bench makes you shiver. You draw your lone brown sweater tight around you. Eighteen months later, you'll visit this accursed bench in your memory. Was it a bench that gave ordinary human beings the power to spy upon their own future?

Freed from the fear of parents and neighbours listening, Ravindra and you get more relaxed about sex. Yet, even as he lies gasping, having returned from the raw red rim of an orgasm smelling of smegma, Ravindra has only one question inside him.

'If I have this talent, will I become famous, is it possible?'

❧ 5 ❧
Death: 2, Life: 0

WHEN YOU RETURN TO BOMBAY, you are greeted by a strange sight. Instead of being in bed at midday, *Nana* is standing at the corner where blind lane meets horse-dung stained road, sucking his *beedi* nervously.

He whispers something to Ravindra, who, forgetting that he's back in Bombay, puts his arm around your shoulder as he whispers, 'Your mother is ill, they want you there.'

You both visit Goverdhan*Bhai*, and while Ravindra appeals to him with folded hands, you stand outside. The mixed and spicy tone of Goverdhan*Bhai*'s reply seals your dream of visiting your village with your artist husband. No, Goverdhan*Bhai* has already done him a favour, subsidising his fun with his fancy English-speaking madam, and who the fuck is to do all the pending jobs, madam herself?

You sense Ravindra's anger at being insulted before you, but all he displays is a tightened jaw.

You are the only unaccompanied woman on the State Transport bus. You stick your hand out of the window bars just enough to touch Ravindra's fingers (how many times will you enact the same scene with different actors?) as the bus leaves, trailing the ripe smell of jackfruit and *kokam* that it has transported into the city.

Your eyes are heavy with cold air, diesel exhaust, *Dada*'s smiling face looming up beside the bus window, covered with coconut soot, light flickering as the night lamps on the highway rush past.

There are sickle-shaped sandpaper slivers under your eyelids.

You expect *Dada* to be waiting near the bus stop on the highway, but there is nobody that morning. Then you realise he wouldn't have known about your arrival anyway. So this is going to be a surprise for him too. You imagine the dance in his eyes when he meets you.

Your shoulder aches as you carry the dowry trunk one kilometre into the village. Already the city has softened your sinews.

You feel like a stranger. After the ten hour roar of the bus engine, the silence is disconcerting, and someone has shifted the vanishing point and the perspective. The village has shrunk diagonally. The trees appear stunted; in the pond a decrepit tractor has attempted death by drowning. Even the light hurts, trapped as it is under a grey ceiling of clouds.

Some recognise you in your six-yard sari, someone notices the bra, your city acquisition, someone whispers. Under Sandhya's influence, you have acquired one more garment, your legless underpants, but nobody will know that. One of your aunts comes rushing out and hugs you: you must have arrived in the nick of time. Someone plucks the trunk off your hands.

Without your permission, your nose is rejoicing in the smell of the cowdung-smeared courtyard, where your father bid you goodbye. But, where is *Dada*?

You rush into the house towards the dark, somnambulist room: your mother must be lying there, waiting. Your aunt stops you, looks over your shoulder.

You turn. There is a crowd of men and women in the courtyard, staring at someone on the ground.

She's lying there, large and ungainly, a carcass chewed by invisible hyenas. Her bones poke into the white cloth. An ungainly reindeer in a *National Geographic* magazine strapped on to the bamboo bier (its spine used to curve for *Dada*, and where is he?) and covered with marigold and *tulasi*.

You rush into her arms and put your ears against her chest.

'What do these idiots know about death? My father courted it. I understand it.'

There, unlike these morons, you can already hear her heartbeat!

'See, she is not even dead. See, all you need is a technique to understand the shorthand of life.'

One soft muscular organ inside you beats for two. Thirty seconds pass before you realise that the thuds you are listening to belong to your own heart.

Your angry wail is a splinter of bone, thrust into your sense of helplessness. When you press her ribcage to wake up her heart, her lungs release a soft, sweet, putrid *whoosh*. When human tissue rots, it rots well.

You want to lie down next to her, smell that smell of coconut, garlic, and acquiescence to an *Aghori*'s experiments.

Go to sleep, forget this happened. She is the only other human being who knew why your father abandoned the family he loved. Why he turned his back on his favourite nine-year-old goddess.

If she had been sent to the city for diagnosis, the X-rays would have revealed the sarcoma. What caused the cells to go berserk? Stress triggered by living like a widow while the husband was alive? Thirty years of oil fumes in the kitchen? Loneliness?

After eight long years, a wound reopens. As they lift the bamboo bier, you clutch her bony feet and do something you have forgotten you ever did. You sob uncontrollably. You cry for her, you cry also for the other memories. *Bhai* feels sorry for you. He draws you back, and, hand around your shoulder, escorts you to the room with the vertical bars that divide space into inside and outside.

Women are not allowed within the cremation grounds, so you are left to imagine the orange tongues tasting epidermis, calcium, plasma, leaving behind an ashy smudge of memory instead of a human being. '*Swaha, swaha, swaha*'... 'Swallow, swallow, swallow'...the chant is a clear instruction to the fire to relish its fleshy mouthful.

Then, as the early June clouds pause for a quick shower over your village, large drops *plop* on the burning wood. Disturbed in the midst of its meal, the fire protests with a hiss.

It strikes you that you would be able to see the pyre from the hilltop. The aunts try to stop you, but you run away. They have always seen you as the product of a mystery, but now you are confirming it with responses unbecoming to a married woman.

The distance between the hilltop and the cremation

ground merely heightens your sense of loss. Tearstains paint lines on your cheeks.

Then, once again, you vanish. You are the cool evening air, you are warm raindrops and you are horripilated skin. You are the grunt of the boar in the bush, you are the lung-billowing fragrance of the wild aniseed bushes, but there is no centre, no you.

By the time you reach home, late in the evening, the hollow inside you is enormous. You are an orphan now, darling, motherless, fatherless, future be foretold, brotherless and husbandless too.

❧ 6 ❧
Death: 3, Life: 0

WHEN YOU RECOVER from the consciousness of your mother's absence, for the next two days, you ask for *Dada*. Did *Bhai* send him to the plateau, on a mission nobody else wanted? Did he go to fetch mother's medicines from a *taluka* town, or from Bombay? And why did nobody ask you, the ace Bombayite? When *Bhai* maintains an irritated silence about your *Dada*'s whereabouts, you interrogate your aunt.

'He was caught playing with a Brahmin girl...with her...' she whispers quickly, pointing to her own chest.

'Caught? Who caught him?'

Your aunt gulps.

'Priest Chintamani saw him first...'

'So?'

'So they beat him, near the ficus near the River Goddess...they say he ran away and slipped and fell head first on the rocks in the river...he died in the *taluka* hospital.'

'Died?'

Your knees are water.

The last thing you remember before you faint are his eyes asking, 'Why must you go?'

A peeled onion under your nose wakes you. When did this happen? Why did they not tell you? When you plead with *Bhai*, he mutters, shrugs, wipes sweat with the muslin towel flung on his shoulders. When you ask him the third time in the day, he loses his calm.

'You and he...you were experiments...unnecessary, dangerous...understand?...we don't want to be touched by the shadow of all that *bhootbaaji* that *Baba* tried...it's another universe...you and he...you just brought bad luck to this family...understand...no need!'

'Not he, not *Dada*. *Dada* did not bring bad luck...he was no experiment... I, yes, was...' speaking as the only one now who knows your father's secrets, '...but you could still have sent me a telegram...'

He snarls. 'We did...you were away in some hill-station...'

Perhaps when your mother fell ill, the villagers sensed that your brother was an outcast within his own home. Perhaps the neutered helplessness against your father rediscovered an easy prey to sink in its fangs. *Dada* had grown from the seed of the man who had shaken the comfortable pillars of the village traditions. The village had shrunk away from your father's alleged mystical powers, and landing blows on the helpless flesh of his wordless son was such sweet revenge. Fear and anger, twin friends of the weak at heart.

Perhaps it was priest Chintamani's way of getting back at you for having made him sin. As a holy man, he had striven to quash thoughts about other women, but your budding white breasts had thrust against the barrier of his

41

subconscious, sprouting defiantly in his muslin dreams. With a single lie, he could ignite a fire against the person you loved most, thus trying to kill that part within himself that he hated most.

Perhaps *Dada*'s death also ended your mother's will to live. You remember her using you to secretly parcel food to him, when your father had locked him in the storeroom for having committed some mischief. You remember her applying warm poultices of turmeric on his wounds, the trophies that announced his triumphs against trees, bees, water, hills. He was the error of her womb; she had to protect him against an unfeeling world.

Perhaps *Bhai* was relieved. He had been the neglected child, despite being the eldest, playing a bit part when he ought to have been the protagonist of the drama in the household. How could a child who lived in the dusk of a sensory world be considered more important than him, the most educated, the sunniest, brightest child of the family? He had read the *Bhagavad Gita* in Sanskrit, not just the Marathi translation, he could recite most of Sant Tukaram's *abhangs*, he could add and subtract and multiply and divide in his head. And yet, his father and mother had devoted their hearts to this...this creature, and this spoilt girl.

He was sure that *Dada* was an experiment, because he knew so little. Your father's experiments had begun because of *Dada*'s birth, not before.

'Your *Bhai* did try to save him, you know,' your aunt continues, 'he ran with him in his arms all the way to the highway, and stopped a truck, and took him to the *taluka* hospital, but it was too late...'

'And did the police ask anybody any questions...or do

they think some castes are beyond such minor formalities? Did anybody else see him touching the schoolgirl besides priest Chintamani? Did the police ask the girl if it was true?'

Your aunt senses your growing anger, but can't explain why nothing had happened.

'He...they...told the police *Dada* was used to being close to you...so maybe he didn't realise how not to touch a girl...and anyway they were just trying to teach him a lesson, they said even your father used to punish him for being wayward...anyway he jumped and hurt himself in the head, it was an accident...only he was responsible.'

'How not to touch a girl.' This, about a brother, who of his own accord stopped hugging his sister when she became a woman.

The village must have succumbed to the convenient outcome of the event. Nobody was scandalised, because to everybody your father had been the scandal, and *Dada* the uncomfortable symbol of his defiance.

Perhaps the only human beings besides you who would have wanted him alive would be the young children in the village.

A shoal of darting, chattering excited boys and girls would chase the two of you back from school, because they knew *Dada* would treat them to delicacies. To them he was the genie who made their wishes come true. He would climb the tamarind tree and drop down plump hard tubes of extreme sourness. There would be a scramble of tiny fingers, red dust and shrieks of delight and then, when they bit into their hard-fought-for fruit, two liquid shocks would erupt from their salivary glands, shoot into the brain and emerge from their eyes as green tears.

And who else could hit with accurate stone missiles the

half-raw half-ripe mangoes on the tall tree that actually belonged to priest Chintamani? The squealing crowd would dive for these gifts: flawless green skin drawn taut around sourness and a soft orange blush of sweetness on top, and a hard core that you flung at other children so they squealed in mock pain.

Then some elder person would bark in anger and the shoal would disperse.

Dada and you, hand in hand, would then skip towards the *paarijaat* tree to collect flowers for *Bhai's puja*.

You butt your head against the walls of the hollow inside you as you wait for the priest on the way to the river. 'Hey, somebody has to be questioned about this innocent slaughter. If my father were here, you wouldn't have escaped.' You shake the *paarijaat* tree with anger, crying aloud for the brother who loved you with everything his tiny heart could hold. White flowers with orange stalks flicker down on you. They flicker on to the memory of a little girl who used to chant in a voice as clear as a bell in a mist:

'*Na me dveshraagow na me loabhmohow, mado naiva me naiva maatsaarya bhava...*'

'I am neither ill-will nor anger, neither greed nor temptation, neither pride nor jealousy...'

You brush aside the sound and the meaning of the chant. You don't want to understand your anger, you want to be consumed by it.

A dark vein thrums in your forehead, but when priest Chintamani finally comes round the bend in the path lined by cacti pointing stubby fingers skywards, dragging the paralyzed left half of his body, the shock of the sight slows your heart. You didn't know he had become half vegetable. Standing there, not knowing what you want to do, maybe you yearn to wrest out something permanent from a situation so suddenly out of hand. When the priest reaches close enough for you to hear his laboured breathing, you hiss at him, blocking his path.

What has overcome you? How dare you accost the seniormost priest? Must be your father's genes...he had not respected customs and beliefs, had he?

'You thought your gods were blind, did you? You thought your gods were separate gods, they would pardon your lust, your revenge, the killing of an innocent boy, you monster, yes, what?'

Priest Chintamani knows you know how he lusted after your pubescent body. You believe he was angry about his secret and ended up venting his anger on someone you loved. You want to lunge at him, shake the answer out of him, but the grapnel hooks of tradition sunk in the flesh of your back are an unbreakable leash.

Unknown to you, many pairs of eyes watch the confrontation from behind the cactus army.

The priest, his tumescence softened by an unidentified paralysis, waits without reaction for you to step aside, then limps away in silence. He has no strength to protest against a woman from a grieving family casting her impure shadow on him, grilling him about a crime his god has already punished him for. The saliva that once left strands of lust on your breast now drips uncontrollably from the side of his paralysed mouth.

When you return home, *Bhai* drags you into the room with the vertical bars on its windows, slaps you, hisses at you. 'Who the hell do you think you are to speak like that to the village priest? Just because you went to a city, you forget the boundaries of decency...of caste? You think you are a goddess...you fool...If you are a goddess, why can't you produce a child of your own, tell me!'

You sit on your haunches, clutching your knees to your chest in the semi-darkness, clutching them hard enough to squeeze and crush the thoughts in your mind. Maybe you are sterile, an empty pod, a dried up fallopian. Maybe you are blessed not by a goddess, but by a ghost. Maybe you are a blind alley in the maze of evolution.

The only man who could even attempt to answer these questions is in flight, pursuing an illusion down a tunnel.

In the absence of his father, *Bhai* must attempt to set his mother's soul free from the net of desire it is caught in for twelve days. The thirteenth day has to be a feast to celebrate its liberation. All the families from the village have to be, and have been invited, and the visitors express surprise at the ease with which you can still bend down and serve everyone non-stop for three hours.

Destined to feed the mouths that maintained a collective silence when the brother you loved most was killed, you refuse to speak to any of them.

Despite your elder brother's wrath, or perhaps hardened by it, next morning, you go by yourself to the River Goddess. Tear drops plop into the black pond of memories. A bamboo arcs, fingers touch across iron bars, a bloodstained stone lets out strangled screeches in protest.

You don't understand why you do it, but you feel the certainty in your spine: so you touch the stone with your forehead and swear to *Dada* that you will never return to this village. He was guilty of nothing except being born in a village where caste could cut your lifeline.

You decide to feed your five senses their final meal.

The rough ringwormed skin of the *gorakhchinch*, the translucent jade hearts of the ficus, the deep pools of Shankar the water buffalo's eyes, the taste of the water that came out of the earth's womb, the cricket's wooden chirr...you hoard the sensations.

'Eat well my five friends, for from tomorrow you starve. I have nothing left here to come back to, and Bombay has nothing for you.'

'*Aham bhojanam naive bhojyam na bhokta...*'

'I am neither enjoyment nor enjoyer, neither am I the object of enjoyment...'

❧ 7 ❧

Songs of the Madder Soil

WHEN YOU RETURN TO MASKA CHAWL, the familiar smell of urine and sickly sweet damp clothes is a comfort.

Mai embraces you, assuring you that she understands what you have been through without saying a word. In the evening, Ravindra takes you to the beach, so you can tell him what happened. As you speak, and weep intermittently, he paints on the canvas of the sky before him.

For weeks on end, he watches your silent sorrow turn into a painting. A giant cloud of leaden grey on the bent back of a matchstick girl, her feet mired in a deep wet orange, a mixture of red soil, crushed *dhak* flowers and anger.

A young boy and girl floating underwater, joined by a cord of sunlight, surrounded by transparent naiads and twin-headed silver snakes, all immersed in a thick river of cobalt.

Another young girl, in beaten-gold armour this time, her hair in flames, holding a sword too large for her, holding it in two frail arms against a pack of wolves. She doesn't realise it, but the wolves are skulking backwards because behind her is an old man in white robes, brandishing rivulets of electricity.

When you first see the actual painting, you gasp and clutch his arm. After a long time, the hollow inside you is filled with light. Ravindra has brought you to his school friend Gajanan's house, and revealed the oils he's been painting secretly.

'Know what I have called the series? "Mayan Magic!" Good, no?'

'Yes, the name is good, and the paintings are breathtaking!' you reply. 'Did you bring my name in deliberately?'

He looks at you, smiles, replies, 'Who else inspires my art?'

Ravindra the artist uses colour with an abandon that would cause Ravindra the human being's heart to implode. For the first time after Matheran, you laugh like a child, as you hug your husband, happy for him, a man who has discovered a true instrument of release.

The moment is charged enough for Ravindra to leap over his inhibitions, for the two of you to make love on the cold floor. He is uncharacteristically rough, wanting to mount you from behind, while he grabs you with turpentine-coarsened hands.

His paint-stained fingers crush shut the lidless pupils on your breasts.

Of course, there is still one shadow permanently accompanying you both, a shadow that flares every time you copulate. Whether it is your dried-prune ovaries or his pockmarked sperm, fact is, you have breasted the finishing line of suspicion by not getting pregnant within months of your marriage.

Your own brother has been ashamed of this slur implied in your failure, remember?

Ravindra is drunk enough on his new-found love of painting to brush aside his parents' discreet queries, but unknown to him, the shadow is growing into a gulf.

He works late nights at Goverdhan*Bhai*'s to be able to afford the canvas and the oil paint, so you see less of him. At home it now smells of linseed oil and turpentine instead of damp cloth and ammonia.

Every time you go out to buy fresh vegetables for the house, you pass a squat building struggling to retain its aloneness against tea stalls and stove repair shops that lean on it from both sides. One morning, consumed by curiosity, you enter the building.

It's a library. Dnyanabodha Vachanalaya. It props its mission of 'spreading the light of education, battling the darkness of superstition' on cupboards. The wooden frames clutch broken glass panes that clutch empty starbursts of darkness in the centre, letting dust trespass on the silence and privacy of the rooms in the minds of *dhoti*-bushshirt-coat and black *topi*-clad sentimentalists and iconoclasts of early 20th century Maharashtra. The feet of the cupboards rest in saucers full of water, to prevent ants from getting into the cupboards.

That morning, the only person there is a myopic old man in white pyjamas and *kurta*, struggling with the library cards. When he sees you, he adjusts his white cap and says, 'What number?'

'No, I do not have a number.'

'Then...why don't you join... It's only ten rupees per month.'

'No... I was just curious... I like books, I didn't know...'

'Can you read and write Marathi...?'

'Yes...but...'

'Do you stay close by?'

'Yes...Maska Chawl...you know, inside the lane...'

'I know Maska Chawl...can you spare time in the afternoon...we desperately need someone to give out magazines and books...we will pay you a small salary...'

The thought excites you no end. While Ravi (you have shortened his name in your mind after Matheran) is busy with his paintings, you can earn some money...no housewife in Maska Chawl does that...

'I'll ask at home...sounds like a good idea...'

'Try...nobody wants to read nowadays...if you like books...maybe...'

Neither Ravindra nor your in-laws show any resistance to your proposal...every additional rupee helps.

So you become a kind of librarian at the Dnyanabodha Vachanalaya. You feel happy and proud that you are an earning member of the family. What more can you expect to be in Bombay, with a Class Five education?

You start making friends with the youngsters who arrive there. Young students, their imagination fired by examples of scholars and architects of a new India who studied for their exams under street lamps, have come to read the newspapers for free.

Soon, like Sanjay and Sandhya, the young men discover the shocking fact that you not only belong to another gender but to another race. You are the Prometheus of Girangaon, Medium of Mill-town Masses. You can translate the language of fire. You can point them to books in a language that holds the key to the known universe. The first effect of this discovery is that the Library Board passes a resolution to order more copies of the English newspapers. The second effect is the dramatic increase in the overall level of informality at the library: for the first time, there is a librarian who is interested in conversation!

You have become the still centre of an excited world. In early July, Mr Mhatre, who hawks the special edition of *Navin Mahila*, a 'female oriented' magazine, strikes up a conversation with you. You mention how 'Songs of the Madder Soil' was your father's favourite, how the meaning has been stitched into your blood by the lullabies you have hummed since you were four.

Mr Mhatre wipes sweat off his prickly heated forehead, and suggests you write a piece about your reactions to the Songs. Urban poetry is likely to be the subject of the next few issues, and a reaction to such a literary milestone from such an unexpected source as you would be hugely welcome. His long, low-jowled face stares at you, you almost expect the canines to stick out when he smiles.

You detect no artifice in this request. It is unusual enough to interest you. You spend one week shaping the piece, handwriting it on ruled paper through an afternoon quiet shredded by the incessant creak of the fan, and hand it over to Mr Mhatre when he arrives next.

Your perspective is heartfelt, uneducated, naïve.

'A poet feels more, but he also sees more, understands more. Is it enough for him to be a "mirror walking down the bylanes" of a mill-town? I think not. After having laid bare the heartlessness of the city, we would have been grateful if the poet threw out lifelines of hope for us unfortunate refugees. It is a burden the poet must carry, only because only he can carry it.'

A month later Mr Mhatre returns with the magazine. You see your article, and are amazed by it. All your life you have only read magazines, you have never been in one. So easy to be published! 'Look, it's you, country bumpkin, commenting on the work of a giant who your father revered.' You carry the magazine home for *Mai* and Ravindra. *Mai* faces the corner abode of the gods, and thanks them. Ravindra mimics the most popular radio station, 'This is Radio Ceylon... According to the latest news reports, Maya Patil has been asked to leave Bombay for blasphemous statements about an icon...'

The three of you laugh while *Nana* snores.

Then you forget about the piece until one rainy evening, a freaky rainy evening a year later. Having nothing to do in the absence of the faceless readers of newspapers, having listlessly nudged the membership cards into vertical discipline for the third time, you walk back behind the cupboards and open two old cardboard crates.

'They were donated by my stupid father...' the voice behind you is a cardiographic flatline. 'He believes the English language is a weapon that today's youth must carry hidden in their sweaty armpits. This was his grand gesture towards the youngsters who joined the mills, the mills that made him famous as a poet.' The young man is card number 339; you have not noticed him as anybody special until now. He stands dripping a circle of sound around himself.

Why are all the turning points in your life linked to rain?

'Varun', 'the God of water' by first name, and 'Khare'

the poet's son, by his second, is wetter than WD-40. You offer him your scented handkerchief, your third city accessory, in the village your *pallu* did the job, and his horsy face opens into a tobacco-stained guffaw. 'Furry tongue,' you note, 'must be poor digestion.'

'Is your father the poet who wrote "The Songs of the Madder Soil"?'

'Yes, and are you the woman who wrote a piece on them in the literary special? I asked their representative, Mr Mhatre. The old man is dying to know who this Maya is...the bastard has never been criticised...serves him right!' You are taken aback by his attack on his own father, but hide your discomfiture behind a weak smile.

Wiping and adjusting his thick spectacles, he guffaws again, this time including a quiet youngster waiting for him at the door.

He smiles at you again, 'You must be the first person to open those crates...he sends me here periodically, to check if the youngsters are reading those dusty donations of his!'

When he gestures, his friend draws closer.

Varun points at you, and addresses his friend, 'Pankaj, look, I found her...the woman who wrote that article about father's poems...bloody hell...he really was surprised...on the one hand Miss Nirmala sucking up to him...on the other an unknown woman puncturing him.'

The youngster, Pankaj, breaks into an innocent smile, making his round face split into horizontal halves, and the two of them find the entire episode far funnier than you can find reasons for.

'Criticise? No, no...I love the songs...'

Your heart races. 'Hope I haven't...' Haven't what?

Haven't inadvertently hurt the poet? And what's wrong if you did? Worried that you had hurt your father too? A vial of remembering gets uncorked, releases faint echoes of *Baba*'s firefly-studded tenor.

When Pankaj and Varun leave, you return to the cardboard crates. Your mind is half on Varun's comments, when suddenly you are overcome by cowdung smells and your *Dada*'s body heat and afternoons preserved in a glass house of silence.

Once again you are sinking your hands in a liquid treasure of words, experiences, stories, responses, once again you are opening a perfumed vault. Père Teilhard de Chardin, Boccaccio, P.G. Wodehouse, *A Guide to the Perplexed,* Rainer Maria Rilke, James Hadley Chase, *Reader's Digest* 'Use the Right Phrase'.

Spores of ideas float across time, lock into the tiny landing stations at the fringes of your consciousness, release self-replicating worms of ideas, irrevocably changing the content of your being. Once again.

'Listen (it is 1960, wives still cannot call their husbands by their first names), guess who I met today? Remember the poems my father taught me, that I sang for you in Matheran? Remember I wrote a piece for the special edition of the magazine *Navin Mahila* about this poet? Krishna Khare? His son. What a disappointing person! Imagine. His father inspired so many people from Konkan to bear the brutality of...'

Ravindra watches you in fascination. He listens to the cerulean blue in your voice get thicker with excitement, but he isn't interested in the wordsmith's son or the poetry. He is busy chasing the ability you told him he possessed. On stretches of canvas he's furiously painting you, first your voice, then your smell, then your smile, verdigris finessing into black segueing into ochre dissolving into a crimson pool of sorrow.

Watching him immerse himself in his painting, you bring home a book you've found in the dusty heap in the library. It traces the life of one of the greatest artists of the 19th century: Vincent Van Gogh. You read out a   paragraph.

'The miner was so badly burned and mutilated that the doctor had no hope for his recovery. Only a miracle, he thought, could save him. Van Gogh tended to the miner for forty days and saved his life. And then a vision came upon Vincent. The scars on the man's face, the man resurrected by a miracle of care, looked to Vincent like the scars from a crown of thorns, a vision of resurrected Christ. Vincent painted him, and then cried, "I am the Holy Spirit, I am whole in spirit".'

You tell Ravindra that you barely understand what happens inside an artist or a poet's mind, but it does appear to be a desirable madness. A madness that leads them closer to god. Ravindra listens in fascination, dreaming of Van Gogh's Arles with its violent colours.

Ravindra and you spend more time at the beach now, more because he has so much to talk about. You too have fallen in love with the tickling between your toes when the water recedes, the subsonic chanting of the sea waves, the colours playing on the water.

Just before the Ganapati festival, one of those evenings, you sense he has reached a threshold. In the half-light, you see him weep silently, for the first time. It's been three years since your marriage, and apparently *Nana* has openly asked Ravindra if he'll ever get to see a grandchild, or does he too have to offer another child's blood?

'What about you,' you ask him, 'do you want to offer another child's blood?'

He stops mid-sentence, hurt, angry.

When you say, 'I'm sorry,' he gets up, walks away, shouts back, 'Oh, shut up, shut up, go and ask that bloody intelligent poet of yours!'

You stare at the sea, which has tiny circles of light all over it because you stare at it through your tears. Who would help? *Bhai* did not want you, the shadow of the *smashaan*, he was happy keeping you at a distance. Even if *Dada* or your mother were alive...they would not understand. Sanjay? Too young. Sandhya? Ditto.

Your only hope in this world is to make Ravindra understand that the two of you would have to solve the problem together: so you get up and look for him in the Sunday crowd on the beach. You practise your monologue. 'Let's see a doctor. And if there is something wrong with me, you may, you may, for your own good, marry again.' Then you add an afterthought that has no answer: 'Maybe, but what if there is something wrong with you too?'

The thought breaks up the beach into flickering coloured balls of light again.

As the night stubs its toe on the dusk, bleeding ink, you sit down on the sand, tired, helpless.

Bombayites often dump their *nirmaalya* into the sea. The sea regurgitates it in disgust, depositing flowers without petals, tapeworms of cotton thread and shrivelled *tulasi* leaves on the sand. Your hand feels some of this detritus, triggering the sadness associated with that smell of dead flowers in the room of gods back home in Wada.

You bury your face in your hands and start sobbing.

You give a violent start when someone puts his arms around you. It's Ravindra. He has been following you at a distance, torn by his own indecision. You blurt out your practised monologue, and Ravindra sees a stony mass of black, burping, with lidless eyes, over a messed up embryo.

When he speaks, his voice is distant, 'Maya...don't worry... maybe I have a purpose in life besides becoming a father...should I not become a famous artist...a successful artist...*haan*? You showed me a new path... stay with me...let me try and talk to *Nana...haan*... okay?'

He's so excited by his new resolve that over the next few evenings he drags you around the Ganapati festival *mandaps*, a festival that uses a benign god for social intervention. The atmosphere is charged with sentiment. Huge statues are surrounded by mannequins that reflect social messages. Classical music concerts, feature films, skits by children make the celebrations larger than life, very different from the quiet homecomings of the Lord in the village.

One of the festival *mandaps* has a blow-up of Krishna Khare, with a legend under it, 'The poet of the masses, Krishna*rao* Khare.'

Ravindra whispers to you, 'One day I'll be there...won't I, Mrs Patil?'

'Yes, but that alone is not important,' you tell him, and you regret saying it, because he grows sullen and asks you, 'So what really is important, Miss Know-all?'

You don't want to confront him just when you have patched up over the lineage issue, so you backtrack, but without compromising your original thought.

'To connect is more important, to connect to others, if you are lucky, to that which we call god.'

He's pacified, but confused and sullen. You return home like a traditional couple, he ahead, you a mere afterthought in a patriarchal society.

☙ 8 ❧
Mriga

A WEEK LATER, Varun, the poet's son, returns to the library with an invitation for a quiet evening get-together.

You cannot resist the temptation of meeting a legend that your own father adored. You want Ravindra to accompany you, but he is neither interested nor free. He is at Gajanan's studio, marrying his instinct to canvas skin rather than the unyielding tin of shop signages, nursing a gigantic secret in his own heart.

He smiles to himself as he imagines your surprise when he breaks his big news that night.

You plead with Sandhya to accompany you, but she has already planned to be at her factory *puja*. Mercifully, Sanjay agrees to accompany you to this mill icon's home. Ravindra seems okay, as long as someone who knows Bombay accompanies you.

The poet's house is many kilometres away. You travel from mill city to Brahmin city, from blue collar ghetto to white collar ghetto, from low town to high town, and when the bus drops you there on that fateful Sunday, too early for the party, your body responds to the extreme closeness of the sea.

As you sit there waiting for the poet in his house, with the sound of waves leaving you drenched one moment, dry the next, you sense a loosening. You remember your father telling you how the sea's embryonic fluids and rhythmic breathing mimic pre-birth conditions, making the mind slip off its moorings. He'd mentioned experiments at an institute, where adults starved their senses, floating in darkened chambers to regress towards their past.

Instead, you bob on the waves towards the present. Your village recedes, your brothers recede, the traces on the pebbles at the bottom of the river dry up.

'Here's Maya. She wrote that essay on your poems. She guards your dusty English donations at that vague library.'

'What do you do, Maya, besides poking fun at my work?' His smiling voice is a mix of marigolds plus razors plus honey.

'Sir,' you think, 'with that voice you could slow the beat of a hummingbird's wing down to five per second. You could make *gulmohars* menstruate before time.'

Despite your nervousness, your reply is unusual. You blurt it out.

'I? I make *chapatis* sir, make memories, make water when my modesty is not a victim of humanity living in pigeon colonies, read Père Teilhard de Chardin donated by somebody...but whatever I do, I do not poke fun at your work.'

Sanjay smiles at Varun, impressed by your reply, still overawed by the occasion.

Krishna Khare replies with a laugh.

'You remind me of Varun's mother. She too loved to

reduce the known universe to palpable boluses.'

He runs his hand over his bald head fringed with white copper wire, an artistic hand, fingers leaning towards the finger of Jupiter.

'Sir,' you think admiringly, 'you are meant to be genetically wise.'

The edge of his laughter is hardened by the snap of thunder.

'*Arre*, Maya has ushered in an illusionary *mriga*,' he says, referring to the constellation that's heralded the monsoon for over four thousand recorded years on the plateaus and coasts of the Gondwanaland plate that butts blind, head first, against the Prussian plate, heedless of whether the Himalaya range wanted brittle mantel thrust up its arse, making them rise two relentless inches per year, creating the ultimate challenge for mountaineers who, swaddled in Gore-Tex, tickle their razor-edge backs.

Today, you seem to have triggered an unseasonal September rain.

Of the other invitees to the gathering only four brave the downpour. A young girl called Nirmala, with a very daring shoulder-length haircut and blackened teeth, who's made Krishna*rao*'s poetry the subject of her doctoral dissertation, and the Gokhale couple. Mr Sadashiv Gokhale is the publisher of Krishna*rao* Khare's poetry collection, and over his cup of tea urges you to write a piece for him. His wife stares at you with an uncomfortable smile, for there is far too much unknown about you. The puffed rice stuck in her teeth makes her smile comical. The fourth attendee is Pankaj.

Nirmala takes you and her *beedi* aside onto the balcony, quizzes you about your experience with poetry, how it changed when it was recited to you rather than read by you.

She is a Communist at heart, she confesses, she hates poets who write flowery stuff. Damn the daffodils. Poetry must be as close to reality as blood and bone, don't you think? Haven't you read Mayakovsky? Don't you believe Mr Khare's poems are like tiny daggers...especially when sung...they can even cut into a conscience covered by layers of capitalist lard, can't they? You've never heard anybody talk so much in your life, and certainly not a woman who stares at you from between twin snakes of smoke rising from the corners of her lips.

Pankaj stays close to Varun the whole evening, taking large gulps of whisky but staring at you and at Krishna*rao* intermittently. When Varun leaves the room raising his little finger to indicate an urge to relieve himself, you feel Pankaj's tug. Sanjay steps closer to you, wanting to protect you. Sanjay, Pankaj and you occupy the tips of an equilateral triangle.

Pankaj smiles and raises his hand to begin a sentence, 'You...' You complete it for him, 'remind you of somebody?'

When he laughs the same guileless library laugh, you admit to yourself he reminds you of *Dada*.

You smile back.

'You remind me of my elder brother...he lived in a special world...do you too?' His face colours for reasons you do not understand.

'I...' he stutters, 'I don't... I just think you have a kind face.' You have never been paid a compliment in your life. You watch him over the rim of his whisky glass, encouraging him to tell you more.

'My sister, she had eyes like yours. She understood everything I did, she never said it was wrong or right, she just...' his voice chokes. The memory of *Dada* mixes with an urge to stop his pain, and you reach out and touch the hair on his bowed head, the first male other than your lawful husband you have touched after your marriage. Varun returns just then, seems to understand Pankaj's state of mind, puts his arm around him, and explains with a smile that turns his pupils into pinpoints behind the thick lenses,

'You know when we men get drunk...we grow sentimental...'

Your foursome non-conversation is interrupted by Nirmala's announcement.

'Friends, let us not forget the reason why we have gathered today. Let us wish Krishna*rao* many years of creativity and courage on his 50th birthday!'

There is mild applause, followed by Nirmala's explanation that a formal celebration is to be held by the Marathi Poetry Society over the weekend, but you were part of the privileged few to wish him first. Various guests greet Krishna*rao* differently, the Gokhales presenting him with a surprise cheque, Nirmala hugging him, you with a polite *namaste* muttering, 'I wish my father was here now!'

When Pankaj goes to him, Krishna*rao* clasps him to his chest, musses his hair playfully and kisses his forehead. 'Thank you for everything *beta. Sadaa sukhi raho*!'

Varun puts on a LP record of Krishna*rao*'s favourite *thumris*, and for the second time in half an hour you are touching a man who is not your husband. Pankaj is staring intently at the sea, and you feel sad. 'You will not understand,' he blurts out, when you whisper pointlessly, 'It is okay, things will change...' Varun joins you and Sanjay in the balcony, puts his arms around Pankaj's shoulders. The four of you form a caucus, exchange banter, unaware of the growing rain.

Behind you, the other guests have already said goodbye.

We spin the web of our own destiny. Spinnerets secrete water-soluble memories, everything from the arboreal man's fear of falling to the lacerations of a father's early departure, and the ooze reacts with the air of the present, everything from a poet's need to be surrounded by admirers to a leaky sky...and hardens into our destiny.

It is 7.30 pm. Inside an hour the apartment building has walked into a flood. Brown waters of the streets cut through sand, rushing down the murky throat of the sea.

'This must be the revenge of the gods that watch over your village, Maya. They have forced me to feed the hand that criticised me.' Krishna*rao*'s voice breaks your huddle. You turn to see him walking around peeling a potato, confident that he is embarrassing the four of you. His laughter is again tipped by the sound of thunder.

You charge into the postage-stamp-sized kitchen.

'Don't be silly...men only cook at wedding banquets.'

'Of course, this is a wedding,' he guffaws again, exactly like his son, '...a wedding of two opposing viewpoints!'

The three young men look at you sheepishly. You stand in the middle of a seesaw. It is ridiculous for you to let a legend cook for himself on his birthday, it is ridiculous that the first time you have come out unaccompanied by Ravindra, he will not know why you are so late.

Within half an hour, with unconscious ease, you have

rustled up a steaming hot meal. At the dining table, Krishna*rao* sits with a glass of warm gold liquid. He looks at you, strangely subdued now. 'Want some?' He then looks at Sanjay, who continues to be tongue-tied.

You shake your head for a vigorous 'No', not knowing what it is called precisely, rum or whisky or something else, but his breath reminds you of the sour smell exuded by the drunks at the State Transport bus stops on the highway going past your village. Varun doesn't seem to share his father's love for alcohol, but he too is quiet. The four men eat silently, lost in their own thoughts. After they have finished dinner, you stand near the kitchen platform (this is the first time in your life; you always had to squat before a fire or a stove) and fluff up a couple of *chapatis* for yourself.

Krishna*rao* comes from behind you, clutches your right hand in his palms, warm and soft as ripe mangoes preserved in hay.

'You asked in your article why I abandoned my Konkan, Maya, I say because we are refugees, ecological refugees, emotional refugees, even spiritual refugees. After a long time though, Maya, I tasted the taste of Konkan, I felt at home...the way you cooked...' The marigolds in his voice are dewy. It's all too sudden for you to react, and you don't speak.

When Sanjay and you go down the steps to leave for mill-town, your heart sinks. The water has risen to the steps. Varun and Pankaj insist that you wait for the high tide to recede, you can't possibly walk all the way back, no buses will be running anyway.

No escape. Sanjay and you sit on the sofa, ill at ease in the silent house.

Varun vanishes into a room, then pops out later, mumbles, 'Why don't you call some phone near your house and tell them you're stuck here?'

You realise you don't remember the number of the telephone at Goverdhan*Bhai*'s shop, and you feel worried about Ravindra.

Suddenly you are all alone with Sanjay in a strange house. Varun has given the two of you pillows and sheets if you want to rest and has burrowed into the darkness in his room, you dare not knock on the door, and Krishna*rao* is adrift on a sea of alcohol-stained dreams elsewhere.

Pankaj sits with the two of you for some time, but the alcohol gets to him, and he mumbles, 'Goodnight, Maya*didi*' and withdraws into another room.

You sit on the Rexine-covered sofa, your mind blank and washed out. The naked bulb drips bile, while in the darkness outside the rain streams down into the spluttering, angry sea. Sanjay has gone out in the rain once to see if there are avenues of escape, and has returned dejected. He sits on a chair, with his head hanging in sleep, shivering once in a while.

You cover him with a sheet, ask him to lie on the sofa.

The rain is a wall that seals in the uneasy silence in the house.

You fight the heavy hand of sleep that's forcing your eyelids shut. You think of *Mai*, waiting for you, Ravindra, scowling like a character in a painting, *Nana*, coughing in protest...you slip into exhausted dreams.

When you emerge out of your stupor, your body clock triggering off the waste in your bowels at four at dawn, you are lying on the sofa adjoining Sanjay's, but covered by a sheet.

When did you fall asleep?

Who covered you, Sanjay, Pankaj, Krishna*rao* or Varun?

What did they see of you in the pale light?

What must Ravindra be thinking?

What must the neighbours in Maska Chawl be thinking?

Sanjay and you do not wait to say goodbye to the three men. You wade through the grey flood. You have to hold Sanjay's hand many times as you push against the knee-deep water. You get into an empty bus and reach mill-town.

Sanjay and you walk into your lane…you are walking in together after a night of absence.

Inside your mind, you are as naked as a baby.

Your bladder is about to burst; you hadn't dared to look for a toilet in the poet's house. Nobody is looking at you as you enter the Maska Chawl. Every household is mopping up the unforeseen changes in their tiny lives caused by the rain, but in your mind every single resident is standing outside, lining the narrow entrance, the staircase, the corridor. You bend down to negotiate the tunnel of long wet flaps of petticoats and saris on the clothesline, then reach your door.

Like all doors in Maska Chawl, it is always open.

Mai is staring at the tea bubbling on the stove. You rush to her side, and clutch her arm. She runs a calloused hand down your back and whispers, 'Ravindra was so worried, he went looking for you in the rain at midnight.'

Nana is still snoring, his circadian rhythm permanently recalibrated by decades of night shifts.

❧ 9 ❧
AWOL

THE STORM HAS SCRUBBED THE CITY clean by evening: every armpit cleaned of garbage, every ear canal scraped of its caked dust.

At Maska Chawl, the sea pushes sewage through the colons of the gutters, it burbles up through the manholes and toilet openings, leaving the tenants fighting murk and miasma.

Sandhya, the young girl who wants to learn English from you, is unaware that you are distracted by Ravindra's absence; she continues murmuring about the surprise she has brought for you.

She has brought you one of her satin gods as a gift. Below it, in her newly discovered English, is the inscription: 'To my lovely elder sister, Maya.'

As the events unfurl, of course, it becomes clear that no god has any intention of saving you from un-intended malice.

By the time Sandhya leaves, the worry has grown into a pain around your middle. Where is Ravindra? You don't want to lose him like you lost *Dada*.

'Should we inform the police?' you ask, unable to bear the lack of reaction from *Mai* and *Nana*, who coughs in reply.

You go in search of Sanjay, to accompany you to the police station. When you reach the dark stone building, your *pallu* stretched tight around yourself, a thin cotton shield against the antics of fate, it's seven in the evening. It is the time of day when one species retreats into itself, and another prowls the earth. The station reminds you of the mill: coarseness of stone building reflected in coarseness of speech, a hardening of arteries, laughter used like a stiletto, stuck between ribs, upwards, its tip making a swift hole in the heart.

The complaints procedure has been created to expand time. There are uncomfortable questions about your likely fights with Ravindra, about symptoms of insanity, about 'other' women in his life, after all, everybody knows that artists paint nudes.

After the first half-hour, the slow-moving glacier of events brushes aside your control, and tears start streaming down your eyes. You weep, though, not for yourself but for the fact that Ravindra is being imagined as a philanderer, a lunatic, violent husband. A faint memory of the turpentine-stained hands and the cold bench in Matheran, where he asked you if his imagination would lead him away from you, swirls in your mind. Both the police officer and Sanjay stare at the table.

When you are back home, *Nana* is drunk. He is too timid to touch you, angry enough to shout at you. You feel you will get him angrier if you move your head away from him, and the tobacco breath hurts you as much as the words.

'I should have listened to my relatives when they told me that your father had sacrificed a young girl to his crematorium gods to beget you, you child of the netherworld...you gobbled up your father...now you've eaten up my son...and I'm sure you're eating up your own foetus...you sterile bitch...*saali*!'

Mai draws you away, shields you with her arm.

What are you to do? One man harnesses unseen strands of fate to drag you out of your mother's tired womb, then leaves you; another swears by god, ancestors and parents to remain true to you all his life, then leaves you; a third believes you are responsible for both.

Amor fati: love of one's fate. Is this what it means? That every moment splits into two, and you have to decide to breathe life into one of two diverse long-chain polymers of probability...and you always choose the wrong one?

A disgusted *Nana* goes off for his walk to the gate of the mill, to drink tea at the stall, to laugh his phlegmy laugh at one-eyed penises and staring tits and bearded pubes.

You are dozing, guilty, confused, helpless, when the sharp smell of turpentine pierces your nostrils. Ravindra holds your face in his fingers and squeezes it hard, pushes your head against the wall, demands an answer.

You gag on your mucus, suck up air in a giant lung with an excruciated, 'Aaah!' This jerks *Mai* out of her diabetic stupor. She stares at you two, asks Ravindra if he wants food. He smiles a vacant smile at her, while he holds your face, she does a silent *namaskar* to the gods, and returns to her stupor.

'Here I was...desperate to tell you that Gajanan has

71

organised an exhibition of my paintings, and you were not here...'

The twin pulls of wanting to punish you and wanting to share his joy with you splits him down the middle. He shushes you and shouts at you intermittently, and despite smelling the familiar edge of his sweat and the heat of his arm against your breast, you are terrified of the distance he has travelled. What had you done wrong? You accepted the invitation with his permission, you even asked him to accompany you...

He is a gill-less human fish gasping for water in a sea of air.

'...I was like a madman, walking in the rain, looking for you, I walked through waist-deep water all the way to Dadar...while you were with that famous poet...all night...with Sanjay...what will the neighbours say...*haan*?!...that I am a *hijda*...that because I can't father a child, my fair wife chases other men?'

The accusation is too sudden. Between sobs you explain how you couldn't escape out of a beleaguered house. 'Please believe me,' you plead, your voice trapped in the stalactites of mucus inside your mouth, 'You are the only human being I can call my own now, I've lost them, my father, my brother, I cut myself off from my village.'

Inside you, you are naked. 'I don't want to lose you, I'm sorry, I will not go out without you again...if this is what it makes you believe...'

The policemen had asked if Ravindra was involved with other women. Ravindra was asking if you were involved with other men.

Down the lane, the Time Office manager shuffles around a figure of eight, tracing and retracing an eternal path of boredom homewards. The storm loses strength, the universe winds down. Then you share whispered apologies to each other, he for his anger against you, you for not getting through to him, and end up making urgent love, despite the presence of *Mai* who has returned to deep slumber.

✇ 10 ✇
Two New Lives

ONE AND A HALF MONTHS LATER, Ravindra's exhibition is an unqualified success.

Even Khandekar, the *Times of India* art critic notorious for savaging young artists, is enthusiastic about this new autodidact. 'Ravindra Patil,' his bloodstained hand writes, 'is an instinctive radical. He has abandoned the uroboric obsessions of the post-Independence adolescents, and pitted his native sense of colour against the pluridimensional needs...'

After the first two pages of the brochure, you stop reading and sigh at Ravindra, 'I wish they had used a *haiku* poet to explain art...the words would condense meaning as much as your colour does.'

When this remark offends Ravindra, it dawns on you that he hates any references to poetry and comparisons between the two fields. You try to explain your remark, it merely increases his hurt.

Thankfully, this miniature stand-off has no effect on 'The Buyers', who, whisked away into a world of 'penumbral luminosity' by Khandekar, write out cheques with a readiness that makes Batliboi smile non-stop under his pitted proboscis. Batliboi is the Parsi who owns the gallery and takes twenty-five per cent of what Ravindra makes.

You meet Gajanan for the first time. He is physically the exact opposite of Ravindra. Fair, stubby, pot-bellied. 'I know Ravindra from school,' he explains to you, 'and I told him, *saala*, when your new wife tells you you can become famous, you believe her, but for so many years I have been encouraging him to paint...no respect for my encouragement!' Ravindra puts his arm around his shoulders, '*Chup re saala*, don't spoil her mood...writers and painters are not equal in her eyes!'

You really don't know how to react. You shrink away, try and smile at all the neighbours from Maska Chawl who have dropped in. This is all too alien for them. Of course, Sandhya has taken the lead in explaining to some of them. 'See, colour is a language...no? When we see crimson on your forehead, it says..."Married Woman", right, and...'

Batliboi proposes an intimate party at Copper Chimney. He insists on Gajanan being there.

The table linen is paper crisp. The water is freezing cold. They must have a fridge in this big restaurant. You reach under the tablecloth and hold Ravindra's hand, half to share joy, half to share nervousness. A crystal nude rinses her hair in the light gushing out of an artfully hidden lamp. Batliboi insists that you too partake; after all, you are the wife of the youngest Indian ever invited to the Paris Young Artists' Triennial, and after all, beer is not alcohol. You do not understand what he means.

Ravindra agrees and nods acquiescence. His smile

looks as stupid as yours: his blood has not known alcohol before. Encouraged by his agreement, you gulp one bittercold gulp, but reject the huge tankard. Gajanan stares at you, frowning, mumbling under the beer foam that Indian wives do not need to drink to be happy for their husbands. He should know. He's been to Paris, fucked the Tea Board girls from India while they giggled high on absinthe, then lectured them on Indian virtue.

Just that one gulp sets up a battle between you and the silverware. The damned fork nestles too heavily in your left hand, things fly out of your bowl, the spoon haplessly chases circular objects around the plate. You feel the warmth of the beer spread like a nuclear explosion in a silent film.

T^o+ 5 seconds.

'Within a radius of 5 kms, shockwaves leave concrete structures flattened...' and nudes glowing, head dizzy, ears blocked. You feel the food rising up your gorge, triggered by an unknown chemical tripwire. You get up, slide out and rush to the toilet marked with blue seashells.

The next morning you vomit again, and you watch *Mai* smile.

Within a day, modern science has confirmed your joy.

Just what was so special about Ravindra's new batch of sperm that it could wake up your Rip Van Ovaries?

Must be a never-say-die triathlete who braved the forests of cilia, the glaciers of mucus, the hillocks of papillae. Must be a sperm that discovered his self-respect the day Ravindra's exhibition was finalised. And why pray does your body react to this new development in the late evening instead of early morning, as the old wives' tales demand? And how did you miss the initial warning signals, the non-arrival of the crow that came every month and made women untouchable for three days?

Ravindra's voice is choked. Fate had lent him a hand. Just when his baby needed it, he'd got enough money for you to have the delivery done at a private nursing home instead of at a municipal hospital.

Dr Shah, of the private nursing home fame, smiles his practised smile, speaking a genderless Marathi while he reassures you with false familiarity, 'Maya baby, after this first examination, I will see you every four weeks until thirty-two weeks of pregnancy, *samzhi*?'

'Then every two weeks until thirty-six weeks, then once a week until delivery. At each examination, we'll record weight and blood pressure usually, and the size and shape of the uterus...'

So when exactly did your baby kick-start its engine of love...while you were making *chapatis*, oblivious to its struggles in a soft pouch of amniotic fluid?

What now?

Without so much as a by-your-leave, inside the warmth of your womb, the ACTG code of your zip-locked genes has sparked off a millennia-old chemical ballet. Your body is on autopilot, busying itself with the task at hand, it cares little for the potpourri of relief and surprise and wonder in your heart.

Nana and *Mai* treat you with respect: *Nana* begins to include you in his tales of childhood valour. 'You must be thinking all I did all my life was sweat in a mill. Ha! When in school I was the undefeated king of all sports. In marbles, I had this *dhabbu* that could crack open the opponent's marbles (not those marbles, ha, ha). In flying kites, bloody hell... I had this special formula made of glass powder and glue...no bloody kite string would match that...they would say, eh, *Nana* Patil is flying his kite today...beware! And my kite-catching stick...ha...no escape, *baba*, no escape from the man who could leap from roof to roof...' And then *Mai* brings his banter to a halt with an apt remark, 'Yes...that's all you've done...fly kites!' You laugh, because the phrase 'flying kites' also means 'telling tall tales' in Marathi.

But they appear to have missed one aspect of your motherhood that Ravindra is obsessed with.

Unknown to and unsuspected by the three of you, snakes of suspicion, slate grey bodies, poison black scales, slither on a mirror in Ravindra's mind.

Did his fair, English-speaking wife really carry his baby? After all, his own father, *Nana*, had been able to have only one child, him, a certain departure from the other males in Maska Chawl. Or was the baby Sanjay's, or of the great poet she loved? Would he ever know?

He rushes to his confidant, his canvas, giving birth to screeching, howling storms of colour inside squares of white silence.

Many lives wait for a resolution at the threshold of your womb.

✽ 11 ✽

The Chemistry of Motherhood

UNKNOWN TO THE REST, you have changed gender. You are now a mother, and mothers of the world have their own code for life. All of you meet in your dreams, hold each other till you sense the beating of hearts like your babies do in their wombs.

In the dream, you hug the 36kg farmhand with a haemoglobin count of seven in rain-starved Uttar Pradesh. As the baby pushes through while she is cutting grass, she lies down for a couple of minutes, her heart hammering, because she is uncertain of the gender of the baby. Then she uses her daily-wage-earning tool, her sickle, to cut the umbilical cord in haste. The supervisor will cut her daily wages of green chillies and wheat dough if he decides she has stopped for too long. She plants one long kiss on its wrinkled forehead wet with sticky black down. After three girls, it is, finally, a male baby. Her mother-in-law will, at last, accept her.

You hug the globetrotter's mistress, swaddled in Burano lace and decadent silks, a poverty-stricken Perugian living off the scraps of a married man. She vows to the acidic green walls of her love suite in Cannes that the tiny fists of her daughter will never beg for mercy from any man.

You kiss the wet nose of a female squirrel, her heart the size of peanut. She runs away from her nest so the barn owl may pluck her in the blackness of the Amazonian night. Thus will she save her two snuffling, unsuspecting babies.

When you return to normal human beings, you are a bit embarrassed by the attention you get. Despite the broken glass pain piercing the cracks in her feet, *Mai* queues up early morning to buy *kharvas*, colostrum of cow, to enrich your diet. *Nana* smiles more, talks more.

'You know, I tell your mother-in-law that she must have wanted a daughter instead of a red-blooded male...tell me how else do you explain this... *Nana* Patil is famous for having drunk a full bottle of hooch behind the mill gate and then walked home straight, but his son gets drunk on a glass of beer...*saala!*... But you make sure you get us a grandson, okay...must be with steel biceps and an iron dick...' His laughter ends in a cough that rattles the fluff in his lungs.

'*Na mrityurna shankaa, na me jaatibheda, pita naiva me naiva maata cha janma...*'

'I am neither fear of death nor divisions of caste... I have neither father, mother nor birth...I am pure bliss,' sings the young girl inside you, yet you disregard the sound and its meaning. You are drunk on motherhood.

You smile surreptitiously as you bite into a tiny half-moon of earth, it's like the earth behind your house in the village, now frozen into a pot holding *tulasi*. The name 'pica' comes from the Latin word for magpie, a bird that is famous for eating anything and everything. You haven't heard of either the word or its origin, but you decide the urge to eat red earth is perhaps your body's way of pleading for iron. Perhaps your baby wishes to have pistons for heart valves, the better to withstand the cruelty of the mill-town.

Ravindra talks so much it makes you suspicious: there is something not quite right, despite that emotional speech of his about the nursing home.

Ravindra is painting an empty mirror frame, the bottom of the oval blackened by rough blood.

Despite the snakebites of doubt, he plans little surprises to celebrate your motherhood, and more important to him, his probable fatherhood.

One day it is a restaurant at the top of Malabar Hill, one day it is a visit to the lavish Metro cinema. He realises that, unlike him, you've never bunked school and slipped into these dark amphitheatres of human emotion. They are giant celluloid replicas of Sanskrit drama, the same story retold, the same catharsis invited, the same shared understanding of illusion as reality.

The movie is a rerun of the classic *Mother India*, and you discover yourself sniffling with the rest of the audience. You realise how the darkness pushes you inside yourself, and yet you are with a thousand other human beings in the biggest cinema in Bombay, mesmerised by the reality unfolding on the screen. What will your child be like, will it be quiet and suffering like Son One, or headstrong and impulsive like Son Two?

What if it is both? Twelve years later, you will taste the bitterness of the correct answer.

There is a protracted discussion on the name of the

baby. July-borns have to have names starting with a particular consonant: it's a toss between *ga* and *sha*. What about the fact that the baby could reflect the dramatic birth of Maharashtra, a new state that now included Bombay? Why not 'Garima' meaning 'pride', for a girl, or 'Gaurav' meaning the same, for a boy?

You smile at such suggestions.

Names must reflect something more, the inside of a human being, not the society outside. What about *Shraavan*, the season of rain? *Shevanti*, the chrysanthemum flower, made up of slivers of the sun? For days on end, there is no consensus. You enjoy the debate, it's so much fun visiting the future, imagining the nature of an unborn child and determining a name for it.

Then on July 1st, Ravindra escorts you to your favourite ice-cream cart by the seaside, and in a quivering voice declares that he must leave India soon. He cannot postpone his departure to Paris.

'Remember Batliboi mentioning at the restaurant that I was the only Indian to be nominated to the Paris Young Artists' Triennial? Well, Gajanan and Batliboi had sent my work to them and now they have invited me to the inauguration and exhibition...perhaps they'll even give me a scholarship...thanks to Gajanan again... You will have *Nana* and *Mai* with you anyway, and since it is not fixed when exactly the baby will arrive, but the Triennial is fixed, it's only a matter of a few weeks, and I'll speak to you on the phone if at all the baby is there before I return, and imagine if I'm a success at Paris, there will be more money for the baby's future...'

As he blurts out his speech, you withdraw into yourself, not wanting to react. You have used this trick before.

For a moment you want to say, 'No, don't leave me... whatever the reason!'

The next moment you understand the enormity of the step for your husband.

You are the one who always wanted him to think beyond a job, didn't you? You are the one who excited him with stories of Van Gogh, didn't you? Now why do you want to hold him back...just so you feel secure?

In a race that upsets many predictions by fate, your husband, once a local sign-painter, has leapt over native critics, sailed gracefully over international hurdles, then, in a gesture of quiet athleticism, has dragged a baby out of a reluctant womb...ha, what more can he want? If you had asked him, he might have told you what he wanted: 'My talent is now certain. My child's paternity is not.

I wish I knew.'

❦ 12 ❦

One Year of Magic

IT'S THE LAST TIME you will see your husband weeping. He clutches you and showers kisses on your stomach. You clutch him hard in return, touch his pockmarked face, his smooth thick hair, but are unable to speak. Your throat hurts from the suppressed sobs.

'I'll be back soon, my little star, my little baby.'

The rain builds a white wall of sound that makes conversation difficult. *Mai* is weeping too, she can't believe her son is going abroad, he can't even speak English like you can, and are aeroplanes safe?

For *Nana* this departure is enough fuel for a thousand nights. Whose son, amongst those that surround him, has ever gone abroad, *haan*? He imagines himself holding centre court outside his mill.

'*Bhenchod*, you should see the air-hostesses...not one of your Hindi film heroines has a backside that tight...two big buns wrapped in silk.'

'*Saalaa* once they have taken your bag and put the tape, *chhodo*, it's gone... you have one chit in your hand, but the bag, nobody knows...'

The blinking aluminium belly of a plane rushes over you and *Mai* and *Nana*. It dissolves in your tears, its sides leave long white hair of light and water floating in the darkness.

It's July as usual, the season of departure. You have no inkling that the first time you will visit the international airport will be to witness the permanent but unannounced departure of your husband from your life.

Everything you lose in life, you lose with the rain.

Maybe your knowledge of that alien language belonging to a fog-smothered country has created this strange relationship between you and the rain. 'Rain, rain, go away, little Johnny wants to play,' says the book of nursery rhymes you discovered in your father's treasure, urging the rains to retreat. On the other hand, the Marathi singer bribes the rain to come again, '*Yere, yere paavsaa, tula deto paisa...*'

'He's gone, baby, it's just you and me now.' You talk to your unborn child in your mind. Later you imagine your son (yes, because that's exactly what the baby turns out to be) listening to all the conversations in the womb.

Two weeks pass by. You have been tossing castor oil at the back of your throat to overcome the constipation caused by high levels of progesterone during pregnancy. Your son hijacks this as the reason to emerge. He neatly folds up his umbilical cord, switches off the lights and prepares to step out before his destined alarm goes off. This sends frantic jabs to your lower abdomen at midnight. You wake up breathless and sweating.

You watch Dr Shah, who has dragged himself out of his slumber on the second-floor of the nursing home, personally supervising the arrival of your modern-day

Abhimanyu. Apparently, in their fervour to measure everything, the illusionists have created a scale for pain, and the highest number of doles is indeed associated with childbirth. You feel the baby tearing down, about to spill out everything, brown kidney beans, shit-heavy large intestine, jelly-fish bladder bag. You'll be hollow below your navel.

Then you hear his cry.

'It's a boy!' says the nurse from behind her smile-hiding mask. Out of drunkenness caused by fatigue and relief, you slip into your mother dream, and all the mothers gather around you, smiling, kissing your forehead, running an affectionate palm along your back, holding your hands.

When you return, you have been dried and powdered, and there is a cotton cocoon next to you.

'One moment we were one, the next we are two. I the woman was full and complete with you inside me. You the man were incomplete and imprisoned inside me.'

'*Na mrityurna shankaa, na me jaatibheda, pita naiva me naiva maata cha janma...*'

'I am neither fear of death nor divisions of caste... I have neither father, mother nor birth...I am pure bliss,' sings a nine-year-old in a chimera of a village.

'That is what the perennial philosophers said,' you sing to yourself, maddened by the act of creating something that never existed before, 'but this is my reality. I am pure bliss *as* mother, not *besides being a mother*.'

You hold him up for an invisible Ravindra to see, as if Ravindra had had no role to play, as if you had breathed life into a rag doll all by yourself. *Nana* has cashed some postal deposit he's left untouched for years, bought calcium tablets for you, Johnson & Johnson soap for the baby. That's the best he can do to wipe the tobacco breath off your cheeks, where it lodged when he accused you of being a man-eater.

He kisses the baby like it is made of glass, asks, 'Have you decided the name...finally...in our times it was easy...just the grandfather's name...*haan*?...but Ravindra had said we should let you decide... Sanjay sent him a telegram...'

'I thought Shraavan was good, but Sharan, meaning 'surrender', sounds better...'

You guess that's because you feel at this moment you have to surrender to life, rather than demand that your dreams be fulfilled.

Roughly eighteen years later, that name will help you surrender your attachment to your own son.

On the third day, just before you are to be discharged, you have surprise guests. Varun and Krishna*rao*. Who told them where you were? The library people? You hear Krishna*rao*'s laughter reverberating in the corridor, and you cannot but feel touched by his generosity.

Just for you, a one-time article writer.

'*Kaai*, Mrs Illusion, is at least the son for real?'

He laughs at his own joke, then hands over a gift, a tiny silver bangle for Sharan.

Nana and *Mai* watch you adoringly.

They cope with the emptiness of an absent son by showering attention on the grandson. They celebrate the twelfth day of his life, his naming day, with as much ceremony as they can muster. It makes you happy to see them charged up, singing lullabies, talking baby talk, massaging him with oil, telling him tales from the

Puraans. You are in no hurry; you have all the time in the world to talk to him.

In his dreams, in your dreams, in the mother dream.

The letter from Ravindra arrives on Ganesh Chaturthi Day, a couple of months after his departure.

'Dearest Maya,

Hope you are happy. I don't know if the newspaper there mentioned what happened at the Triennial. It was very encouraging. Half of my paintings were sold. They even found my inability to speak English exciting (the French get very excited very fast!).

Jokes apart, they thought I had created a vocabulary of colour that was very rooted in India. They found the use of some colours side-by-side absolutely unbelievable. They say they respect cultures that do not imitate other cultures. I do not believe that all this is happening to me, a sign-painter who happened to marry you. It is all like a dream.

Imagine, next week we will visit Arles. Arles...where you told me Van Gogh discovered the colour of divinity. Sometimes I wonder where you learnt to think the way you do.

I am dying to see the baby. What have you named him anyway? Hope he is fine. Does he look more like you or me? Can you get him photographed at Ajinkya and send me a copy...'

Then comes the sentence you hoped wasn't coming.

'...They have granted me a scholarship to stay here for another eighteen months. Gajanan had been working at

it for some time. And it has come through. As you said,
maybe I'll learn to connect better! I hope you don't
mind. I thought of getting you and the baby here, but
Mai *and* Nana *will be alone. Also the scholarship will*
not be sufficient for all of us. What if the baby falls ill?

Are you still reading all those books I don't
understand? That is meant to be a joke, okay?

Look after yourself. My pranaam *to* Mai *and* Nana.
Please send me the photos.

Your darling husband
Ravi.'

You are happy that he is happy. You are now sure he will
really discover a new universe within himself, he will learn
to connect. You write back a long letter. And you convince
Mai and *Nana* to accompany you to Ajinkya Photo
Studios. It is the second time in four years that *Mai* has
extracted her special sari, considerably upping her average
for its usage over the decades. *Nana* wears the black cap
so reminiscent of the poets of the earlier century.

You like the cocktail of sensations: the female
assistant's slightly warm finger adjusting your face, the
smell of the developing solution that fills the studio, the
feel of the satin on the seats, the regal manner in which
Sharan finally sits on the sofa, waving his short arms, and
then gets startled by the flash bulb.

This is the first and last time in your life that you will
go out with your parents-in-law. All three of you sit at
the beach, the same beach where your husband asked you
when you would loosen the drawstrings that tied the
many petalled mouths of your fallopian tubes. You eat
bhel, drink coconut water, and reach home heavy with

nostalgia. You post the photographs and the letter.

Sharan soaks up your attention every moment. The change of gender into 'mother' affects your sleep. Instead of the deep silk slumber you are used to for all these years, including that shameless thigh-displaying night when you slept at the poet's house, you are now a hair-trigger 100-metre-runner-at-the-Olympic-starting-blocks sleeper. The slightest change in Sharan's breathing makes you fling off the sheets of drowsiness.

The day he learns to smile, the day he learns to turn over, the day he learns to crawl, all of them become milestones that rush past. Almost without thinking, you have begun humming, '*Manobuddhi ahankaar chittaani...*' to Sharan when he lies face down on your extended legs snuffling himself to sleep.

All too often you rest your back against the wall, and slip into short dreams while the afternoon buzzes around you, butting itself against windowpanes of memory.

As mothers, *Mai* and you grow closer. *Mai* tells you stories of her childhood in her village. Marriage at puberty, a long pilgrimage to Kashi, the village demons with extendible arms, the terror of living in a city with a strict mother-in-law. Once you even catch yourselves giggling like adolescents, when she talks about her brother-in-law mistaking her for his wife in the darkness of Maska Chawl. Somehow she speaks as one who looks back almost with fondness, as one who is happy closing her book of life. 'You know Maya, in our generation, it was enough if your husband looked after you...if your children survived...and look at me...I wanted many children, but somehow we didn't manage more than one...but look at the one son I have...he is in foreign...and look at you,' she reaches and touches your face... 'all these new daughters-in-law have so many ideas against their mothers-in-law...but look at you...you treat me like your mother...and then this baby...Sharan...' she says as she massages him with coconut oil, the omniscient medicine of the Konkan coast, '...doesn't even cry...so quiet...tell me what more do I want...? All I want now is that if I die I must die with my *mangalsutra* on...I have no desires left.'

Embarrassed by her compliments, you try to distract her with your observations. 'Do you know *Mai*, when you are concentrating, you stick your tongue out of the corner of your mouth?' She slaps your knee while she giggles and covers her face with her *pallu*.

Wouldn't it have been great if your mother and *Mai* had lived together? They knew so much more about living.

It is during one of those afternoons that Mr Mhatre, the bloodhound from *Navin Mahila*, reaches Maska Chawl. He is accompanied by Sandhya, who, in sheer awe, is almost about to recreate you as a coloured-bead goddess on her velvet backgrounds.

For a moment, out of context, you do not recognise him. *Dhoti*, *kurta*, black *topi*. The prickly heat carpet patch on his forehead unlocks your memory.

'Please madam it is a great honour to invite you to the Marathi Poetry Sammelan in Nagpur, you will be an honourable guest sponsored by our magazine. The Sammelan will be held after Diwali.'

You stare at him.

'Me? Why me? I just wrote down one opinion about one book of poems...I do not know anything about any other poetry...I have studied only till Class Five...'

He interrupts you with an altogether oily smile: 'No madam there are many influential people who believe your contribution is vital.'

'What contribution?'

For some reason, *Mai* interrupts.

'Maya, why argue so much? If they think you must go, go! Look at us, we have not been outside Bombay ever since we came to your village...how nice... Ravi famous for his painting, you for something else!'

Emboldened by *Mai*'s unexpected help, he continues, 'Also, I hope you can rejoin the library, they said they want you to come back at least for a couple of hours per day, please. They need someone who loves books. In your absence, the poor old trustee has to sit there, with his weak eyes, and he can barely cope. They will increase the salary to 200 rupees for you.'

Mai and *Nana* are speechless with pleasure, addicted as they are to becoming the centre of attraction in Maska Chawl.

A son who hops across continents, a daughter-in-law so clever she is importuned by publishers to attend conferences and join a library to save its wealth, and, though neither Ravindra nor you knows it, as predicted by the astrologer in Room 16 on the basis of the sun's position in the birth chart, a grandson who will achieve fame in the arts or music.

❧ 13 ❧

Half Circle, Full Circle

IN YOUR 'MOTHER DREAMS', the farmhand from the Uttar Pradesh village returns. The sickle slips from her hands as she floats upright against the sea of lemon yellow mustard, and waves and smiles at you. 'Great going, sis, work is the juice, hope your city does not look down upon it.'

The thought of drowning your son in a sea of letters excites you.

It does not matter to you that he is only a few months old. Sharan loves the silence and the sun in the library. He sleeps or stares at the patterns that the sun casts on the walls or crawls under the benches.

The youngsters at the library react to his toothless smile and pond-black eyes.

They are your eyes. Inside them are whispering snakes and a dead brother.

Unfortunately, things at home get worse. The cracks in *Mai*'s feet do not heal. In fact, when she stubs her foot, the wound flares, and her right leg grows huge. You have a vague idea that there could be something more serious, but your attempts to get her to meet the oily Dr Shah are fruitless. 'It is enough, Maya, to have seen so much in my sixty years...so long as I die with this *mangalsutra* and my bangles on, I need nothing more...let's spend the money on our Sharan instead.'

The Diwali is low-key, though *Nana*, by his standards, has splurged on his grandson. You make *Nana* and Sharan crush the metaphorical demons of bitter fruit together, and there is widespread appreciation of the traditional sweets you've made.

But you miss Ravindra.

Then, despite the pain, *Mai* makes *laddoos* with raisins and sesame, *laddoos* with ingredients that will replenish the 'heat' that you have lost in giving birth to Sharan. Also, the plateau can get freezing cold, and your frail physique could do with these furnaceballs when you go there for the Sammelan after Diwali.

Nagpur is halfway across the subcontinent, and the two-day train journey across flat land carries you further away than you imagined.

Unknown to you, the postal department has intervened in the story of your life. Two separate missives have arrived. One is a letter from *Bhai*, inviting you to his wedding. Another letter addressed to *Nana* and *Mai* with stamp showcasing the Eiffel Tower, which the Parisians initially called an ugly lamp post, has completed its secret journey across the seas.

The first one you will read after you return, but the second is being read in a slow deliberate manner by *Mai*, her mind trying to create meaning out of the accusations.

Unable to confront you or accuse you directly, unable to confront his doubts about his own sterility or confirm them medically, Ravindra has finally discovered the courage to explain to his parents why he left when he left.

Not because he was late for the Triennial, not because he would lose the scholarship, but because he could no longer tolerate a wife who may have given birth to a child not his own.

Mai hides the letter from her husband because she does not believe what she has read. This one act postpones your departure from the Patil household by some weeks.

Meanwhile, you watch another train drilling through darkness. Box after box of light trundles past, carrying sons away from fathers and vice versa, daughters away from mothers and vice versa, everyone away from everyone else. Steel cages lined with friable dreams.

How far will your train carry you?

For the first time after the Matheran trip you feel weightless. Your senses open up, petals responding to chemical triggers. As you move away from the coast, the micron-thin mucus membrane in your nostril dries up, and the lip edges pull back when you smile at Sharan, who has been fascinated by this new miracle: everything moving backwards out of sight.

You bury your nose in his monkey cap, inhaling the bouquet of coconut oil, talcum powder and Johnson & Johnson soap, your bloodstream thick with oxytocin, the chemical soup of togetherness and motherhood.

It's heaven.

❧ 14 ❧

The Poetry of Pain

THE 35TH POETRY SAMMELAN begins with a hum of expectancy. The President of the Sammelan alludes to the tectonic sociological changes ushered in by the birth of the new state of Maharashtra, the concomitant Mohorovicic Discontinuity in Marathi literature, the challenge before, and the responsibility of, the writers and poets, mirrors of society.

During the lunch break you detect another subterranean activity, but you are unable to unravel the mystery behind the stares. 'Hey, I'm not anybody special,' you say with your eyes, 'I'm just another participant in this Sammelan, invited by a magazine that published my article two years ago. I don't even know why they did so...*hmmm*?'

Has Krishna*rao* slyly paraded you as one more conquest, filigreed moth with eyelashes fluttering to creative flame? Is that why he's included you and Nirmala, the daring PhD student who emits snakes of *beedi* smoke, in most of his publicity photographs?

The painful answer you discover over ragged conversations is 'Yes'. You are one more unsuspecting victim. He got you invited in the first place, courageous poet encouraging fair-skinned, deep-eyed, attractive female critic.

He was not interested in what you said, but how you looked. He was the one who made the magazine sponsor you. You try to stay away from him, but it's too late now.

While your mind is busy coping with the shock, without permission, your senses have floated back to your childhood, bobbing on a sea of familiar smells, though the coast and the plateau differ in the colour of the soil and the taste it lends to all that grows there. The *jowar*, the *brinjals*, the spices reflect the harsher sun of the plateau and a cook with a coarser culinary vocabulary, yet your sense of smell is spitting sparks, hissing, connecting. There is no sweat due to the dry air, but a tiny blob of mucus at the tip of your nostril is testimony to the power of the spices.

It's time for the poetry reading session, and you are importuned to be on stage, though in the row behind. Krishna*rao* has planned a few shocks more for you and the audience. The poet who chronicled the despair of the ecological refugees of the coast, who captured the bittersweet rhythms of the pain of social change, who was revered in Ganapati pavilions through kitschy photographs, has, as it were, turned into an irresponsible, self-indulgent hedonist.

In a dramatic reversal of stance, Krishna*rao*'s poetry is celebrating the sensuousness of the female body. Smooth white thighs like the pith of a banana plant. White tits like steamed *modaks*, that traditional sweet with fluted edges and stuffing of jaggery and coconut (on the coast) and dry sweet flour (on the plateau), the soft white biteable *karanji* of Venus on a human palm.

Before he reads the poetry, he turns and smiles at you.

You are terrified by what the smile suggests to the world.

'My willing accomplice in exploring the landscapes of flesh.'

You rush back to that rainy night, the colour draining from your face. You imagine Krishna*rao* attempting to cover you with a bed sheet, rocking in his whisky-laced stupor, staring at your thighs. 'No, it's just my distorted imagination, that's not what happened. I am not his accomplice. It's all smoke and mirrors.' You draw the sweater tighter against you, wanting to protect yourself not just against the cold.

The slimy threads of that night have snared you and dragged you, against your desire, into quicksand. One stupid night, hunted by rain.

The form of his poetry is as unexpected as the content: the Japanese *haiku*.

Where meaning walks the tightrope of seventeen syllables.

Krishna*rao* has attempted what nobody in Marathi poetry has attempted before.

The *Vidharbha Times* reports a violent reaction. A poet who'd publicly criticised the tragic price of Nehru's socialist machinery was now himself a caricature, leaking the jism of senility. Instead of lending voice to the pain of the masses, he sucks the breasts of physical pleasure. The critic, a sentimental follower of Krishna*rao*, is deeply hurt by this apostasy.

'Has his flock of female admirers cut his balls off?'

He compares the all-time favourites and the recent parodies.

'Feed the hollows in your belly

lullabies of cotton
If your hunger can't feel the difference
neither will your son.'

Vs

'Snake tongues lick
Smooth white pith of your thighs
Lick
The fruit of a million sighs.'

Nirmala, the PhD student, provides a fitting reply the next day. Even on stage she refuses to put down her *beedis*. Most invitees are taken aback by her erudition. She quotes freely from critics of literature and authors alike, from within India and without.

She alludes to Edmund Wilson's hope for synthesis between romanticism and neo-classicism. Why, she argues, can't the same poet reflect the antipodes of not just poetry, but art itself?

'When the Sammelan President speaks of Discontinuity, you applaud. When a poet actually has the courage to explore that Discontinuity, you hide under the petticoats of conservatism.'

Krishna*rao* grins. His one admirer has blunted the critics. What about the other admirer? Mr Mhatre from *Navin Mahila* insists on including your comment. You decline. You are preparing to run away. You don't want to be part of this quarrel.

During one of the tea-breaks, Krishna*rao* corners you with a broad smile and a voice like warm honey pouring on your skin, 'What do you think, Maya, my beautiful first critic, did the poetry rise to your expectations now? Did I not open a new way of looking at sensuality and life? Did I not provide more answers than questions, *kaai*?'

You greet his questions with a nervous smile.

Krishna Khare may be writing dramatically different poetry, but for you, he is a human being scribbling on water. His goal seems to be the altar of success made concrete by the worship of young women, rather than a shared pilgrimage of understanding.

Six months later, you will change your opinion even more dramatically.

There is a guided tour to Ramtek, the six-hundred-year-old temple with half-open eyes. You are not aware that Nirmala and Krishna*rao* are both in the vicinity. Nirmala comments to the group on the proximity of Kalidasa's memorial and Krishna*rao*'s poetry session, drawing parallels with Vilom, the famous counterpoint to Kalidasa.

You hurry clockwise around the temple, carrying Sharan on your hips instead of letting him practise his new found skill of walking, then go and sit in a quiet corner, leaning against a wall, staring at the horizon over your folded arms. You want to feel cleansed of what Krishna*rao* has done to you without your permission. From now on, you promise yourself, you will not believe the obvious.

'On dark nights,
my nails bury half-moons of desire
in your flesh.'

You close your eyes against the afternoon sun, then float away on a sea of sensations. After a long time, you vanish. Worms of red light dance behind your eyelids.

100

The roughness of the stone wall seeps through your sweater. The sound of the bells expands in concentric circles, enveloping you. Sharan runs up to you and kisses your exposed midriff, like fish nibbling your feet in the river in your village.

A voice snaps you out of your nothingness, '*Maate, bhikshaa*!'

'Mother, alms!'

You turn with a start.

You have heard this voice before. A voice buried under an aeon's sediments. A voice burnt charcoal black by the bitterness of sacrifice, untouched by fear of gods and demons, studded with sparkling fireflies.

You shade your eyes against the sun, to see better, to confirm your ears' information. Muscular, ash-smeared body, matted hair. The *saadhu*'s face is hidden by his beard, yet you detect momentary surprise in his eyes.

Eyes that can pierce the veil of the future.

You whisper fiercely, unknowingly, urgently, '*Baba*!'

He does not wait for your alms, and by the time you have looked around for Sharan, plucked him off a stone monkey and rushed in the direction he has gone, the *saadhu* is part of the crowd.

You spot him for a moment, shout, '*Baba*!' and break into a run, Sharan bouncing uncomfortably on your waist.

In response to your cry, Krishna*rao* appears from behind a temple on your left, laughing his purple cloud laughter. You hear Krishna*rao*'s voice, purring in pleasure before his gaggle of admirers, 'Easy, easy, Maya, you don't have to run after men, they will always run to someone like you.'

You turn and walk towards the bus, breathless, angry, disappointed.

Could it have been your father? Maybe it was just another man with a voice like your father's, an innocent man scared by your remark, by a madwoman who sees her father in every old man. Maybe it was your father, walking around India, visiting temples, searching for sanctuaries of light.

Did it shake his resolve, seeing you with a child, probably his grandchild?

You wish that man were indeed your father: you could have asked him to confront his favourite poet. 'Look, *Baba*, his talent eased the pain of thousands of men who were grist to the mills of the city, but does that permit him to treat even one woman like a chattel? And the woman is your own daughter, look.'

You imagine your father burning up Krishna*rao* Khare, like a powerful ascetic from mythology, by merely staring at him. *Whoosh*!

When you sit in the train that will carry you home, you are still covered with the unsolicited slime of stares, smiles and winks. You weave and whisper out stories for Sharan, as he suckles you. The train is rushing towards Bombay, but further and further away from your home.

'*Na punyam na paapam na saukhyam na dukham, na mantro na tirtha na deva na yadnya...*'

'Neither virtue nor vice, neither pleasure nor pain, neither...' sings a girl as she holds her *Dada*'s hand, and returns home at dusk, kicking dust to make red smoke float up the sun's rays.

'My dear Sharan, it's neither virtue nor vice, neither pleasure nor pain...'

Unknown to Sharan, his pilgrimage has begun too.

❧ 15 ❧

Bye Bye Love

SHARAN AND THE DOWRY TRUNK feel heavy as you enter the grey light of Maska Chawl. It's late morning, so *Nana* is awake, but surprisingly, *Mai* is asleep. You kneel next to *Mai* and touch her forehead, she whimpers.

Nana coughs a wet cough. You realise *Mai* has a high fever. She wakes up, dragging her huge leg up with her hands. You push her back onto the sheets, and set about washing the slime all over your mind by the simple tactic of immersing yourself in antiseptic quotidian tasks.

For the next few months you take over *Mai*'s role. You buy the milk from the state-owned milk booths against an aluminium identity card, fill the water when it trickles out of the community tap, drumming its high-pitched rhythm on the copper bottom, cook lunch and dinner on the snorting kerosene stove after unclogging its sinuses with a pin, light the lamp for the gods who have decided to watch the antics of their children with indifferent smiles frozen by cheap four-colour printing.

It makes you feel good that after so many years *Mai*

can rest most of the day. Sharan has begun to speak already and *Mai* has time to teach him songs that she must have sung for Ravindra.

When you read the letter announcing *Bhai*'s wedding, you decide you cannot afford to leave *Mai* alone. She has been your mother since your marriage, and you are not going to abandon her. Once is enough.

But you cannot help think about *Bhai*, the last member of the family you were born in. Did he not deserve your love? Just because he hated being part of a family that was abnormal by his standards! Had the difference in age created this chasm, or was it just you being cussed, blaming him for *Dada*'s death? You write him a letter explaining how seriously ill *Mai* is, and send a sari as a gift for his wife through a distant relative.

You also decide to write to Ravindra about *Mai*'s condition, but when you mention this to her, she shrugs it off, saying it is better you do not write. The quivering hoods rise once again in your mind: something is travelling towards you, you don't know what.

You still have enough energy to be at the library for three hours in the afternoon.

The students look after Sharan, call you *Tai*, lay small gifts of essays and poetry at your feet. You brush off their admiration, yet you cannot but share your enthusiasm for things you yourself read at an impressionable age. You allow them to travel with you to unknown worlds.

On a particular Saturday, after the students have left, you notice a familiar face, but are unable to stick a name to it.

The round-faced youngster approaches you hesitantly: 'Pankaj, Maya, it's me, Pankaj...Varun's friend, we met the year before last at Krishna*rao*'s house...'

All your memories of *Dada* come rushing back, and despite yourself, you reach out and clasp his hand. You realise at that moment that you've returned from Nagpur with your anger tightly plaited with your sadness, and need someone to talk to. You could do with a few of those evening visits to the beach with Ravindra, those quiet uncorking sessions.

Pankaj explains that he'd been dropping in at the library to meet you, for a year now. He always wanted to meet you, but especially so, after the Nagpur visit. He realises now why you were off work. He remarks on Sharan's eyes and smile, congratulates you on the birth of such a happy, good-looking son.

He sits across the partly Rexine-covered table, listens to your experience with his chin in his palms. The afternoon sun bounces off the floor, edging your face with gold dust. The fan creaks away, wearing out Pankaj's silent defence, till finally his eyes are brimming with tears. You mistake them for a reaction to your humiliation, but when he abruptly gets up and walks away, realise that he is grappling with private demons. He returns as abruptly.

Then he takes the plunge, his eyes growing hard, prepared to get hurt, 'You know...Maya*didi*...how similar we are?'

You smile, aware but uncertain of his attempt to forge a sisterly relation. You don't want to get too close to men, after Krishna*rao*'s underhand trickery. No more falling for the obvious, remember?

Pankaj gulps and continues, 'You know Maya*didi*... that some men prefer to be with other...men?'

'To avoid being attached to women, you mean...'

'No, I mean sexually and emotionally...'

'Oh, you mean homosexuals...'

'You know them?!...'

'No! I mean I know what it is about, I've read it in books,' you break into an embarrassed smile, '...but I haven't met a homosexual.'

'You've met three...actually...maybe two homosexuals and one bisexual...'

Despite your own bruises, you listen to Pankaj's story.

Of Varun and him being caught fondling each other as adolescents by Varun's father and famous poet Krishna Khare, of Krishna*rao* blackmailing him, of Krishna*rao*'s increasing demands on his hairless body, especially after his wife's death, of Varun watching and listening to it all helplessly, Varun's deepening hatred for his father, Krishna*rao*'s brutal punishments for his own son, Varun's mental castration, and the final uneasy *détente*: Krishna*rao* has had his fill, younger women have rediscovered him. Now if the two boys won't talk about him, he won't talk about them.

Poet paladin, ecological refugee, politically correct exploiter: he uses both men and women equally skillfully.

Pankaj's voice is like a little boy's, 'You have not met them...but only my Aditi*didi* and *Maavshi* know my secret...and now you...'

Who is Aditi, who is *Maavshi*?

Your *tete-á-tete* has cast a long shadow over the afternoon. The *dhoti*-bushshirt-coat and black-*topi*-clad sentimentalists and iconoclasts of early 20th century Maharashtra, nestling in the library cupboards, are snoring.

When Pankaj gets up, he hands over a tiny chit of

paper. His phone numbers.

'Maya*didi*, at Krishna*rao*'s house, I told you you remind me of my sister, Aditi*didi*...because you listen without making me feel small. When she needed me, I was not able to help her. If you need me, remember this...'

You will not have to wait too long: Within days, a dark lie, unknown to you, will sink its fangs into ankles, poisoning minds, uprooting you, setting you off on the refugee trail once again.

That night, *Mai*'s skin is hot enough to burn your palm. You sit up next to her constantly changing the cotton strips dipped in saline water placed on her forehead. As she travels back and forth between stupor and semi-consciousness, she calls out for Ravindra, and you ask her if you should indeed try and call him on the phone and ask him to come back.

She sniffles, saying no, it's okay, as long as she is with Sharan she is with his image anyway, she's certain.

'Don't be hurt by Ravindra's stupid accusation...even a blind man can see Sharan is Ravindra's son...'

When you decipher her delirious mumbling, a shiver runs up your spine, the hair on the nape of your neck is upright.

Your sleep-starved brain begins to lugubriously link the words and the events, and then finally, in the effete light before the insensitive gods, the jigsaw puzzle starts clicking into place. Ravindra's desperate flight before Sharan's birth, his ambivalence towards your pregnancy, his demand for Sharan's photographs... 'Don't be an extremist,' a part of you fights back, 'maybe it's Gajanan, who can't make up his mind whether to hate women or screw them, not Ravindra, who believes this.'

Nana stares at you with bloodshot eyes, so you ask him if he wants to bring Dr Shah home. When the doctor does arrive at three am, *Mai* is in a coma. The doctor hisses at you for your negligence, you don't have the energy to explain.

Sharan wakes up crying, having lost his pillow of heartbeats. Outside the door, Sanjay and Sandhya appear out of the gloom. Sandhya picks up Sharan, thumps him to sleep on her shoulder. The poison spreads relentlessly inside *Mai*, smothering, choking, snuffing out consciousness.

Death speaks again. 'Fuck you life, I told you I would hunt you down. My minions know every trick in the book. They can crush bone, dismantle joints, release poisons with no known antidotes.'

Mai stays in a coma for forty-eight more hours. You burst out sobbing, unable to watch her go, unsure if *Nana* knows what she knows.

Your mother died with the secret of your birth rotting inside her, what about the truth of your son's birth? Will the burden of battling betrayal be back on your shoulders?

When *Mai* dies she will visit the mother dreams of other youngsters.

For the first time, you are thankful that Sandhya is close to you, holding you tight, weeping for you, nobody's done that since *Dada* at your departure from the village. Sanjay advises *Nana* not to hold up the cremation for Ravindra to return, for it is not certain if he will get a plane ticket immediately, even though he goes off to send a telegram to him.

Instead of the big-boned reindeer it carried many years ago, the bamboo bier wears the weight of a bloated gazelle; instead of riotous cancer cells, this body is full of pus. The drizzle wets *Mai*'s huge *kumkum*, making her forehead bleed painlessly. 'As long as I die with the *mangalsutra* and my bangles on, I need nothing more...' That was her humble demand of life, and she had got it. She sways gently out of sight round the corner of the lane, where many aeons ago, *Nana* told you about your mother's illness.

Sharan weeps with you, for he has never seen you like this. You try to make him sleep on your stretched legs while you drift, your head against the wall.

The house is silent.

The light tiptoes backward out of the room, unwilling to be witness to the naked violence that will now unfold.

You wake up with a start. The topmost copper vessel has fallen off its three-tier minaret.

Before you can snap out of your stupor, you see *Nana* swaying above you, and you smell the stench of raw liquor and anger. The water from the fallen vessel is spreading along the floor, so you stand up and sidle along the wall. *Nana* cannot muster enough courage to touch you physically, so he flings a broom at you.

Its aluminium wrapping catches your cheekbone, but the real wounds are caused by the flesh-searing acid of his accusations.

'You whore, you *raand*, you fooled my son, you fooled me, what did *we* do wrong?'

He bursts into a sob.

'Why didn't you eat up this fucking progeny of your poet like you ate up your brother, you think we didn't know what appeared in the Nagpur newspapers, you bloody *chhinaal*...'

The broom is followed by the bangle that Krishna*rao* gifted Sharan, the newspaper that carried your photograph along with Krishna*rao*, and then, the most crucial evidence in this court of injustice, Ravindra's letter. *Nana* has been calculatedly accumulating the objects of his hatred.

The letter flutters down towards the water spreading in the room, and despite your fear, you pick it up before the words can dissolve in water. Ravindra's belief that Sharan is not his son.

As *Nana* lurches towards you again, Sanjay steps between you and him. *Nana* shoves him away, roaring at him, '...don't touch me, you *maadarchod*, you have been waiting to fuck her too. You look at her again, and I'll pull out your pubic hair one by one...ask your lipsticked whore of a sister to sleep with me. I'll teach her how to tickle cocks...'

You have been unconsciously inching towards the door, Sharan wailing on your hip. Sanjay stands at the door, white-faced, breathing hard yet paralysed, his anger destroyed by the shock of *Nana*'s words, the sanctity of his relationship with you reduced to human dung within moments.

You hand over Sharan to Sandhya, bend down, pick up the broom, and to your own consternation, hand it over to *Nana*.

'Let this end, like *Dada*'s life ended.'

Nana swings it again and again, losing his balance, bringing down the clothesline, hitting your upraised arm, breaking your bangles, tearing your blouse at the shoulder, bruising your ribs, pushing you, shoving you, forcing you permanently across a threshold.

Your departure from the Patil home is unceremonious, uncouth, undignified.

When you trip and fall on your backside, the backside a painter had grabbed many times with unbridled passion, the community footstool in the dark passage smashes into your ribs.

Exhausted, *Nana* flops on to the wet floor, blubbers, calls out to *Mai*, calls out to Ravindra. Then, for the first time in years, he falls asleep before midnight.

'Stay with us, *Tai*, stay with us,' whispers Sandhya, as she kneels beside you, wiping the blood off your forehead with her *pallu*. You shake your head in a firm 'No', aware that you will still be within range of *Nana*'s anger.

Inside you, doubt is extinguished.

You had confronted the village priest for love of your brother. You must confront something more for the love of your son.

Sanjay stands guard while Sandhya packs your clothes into your dowry trunk.

You need a sanctuary before you take your life in your own hands. Just till you can fight back.

You pull out the phone numbers given by Pankaj from your tiny Rexine purse. Two sequences of six digits on a wrinkled piece of paper will now open the combination lock on your future.

When Sanjay returns with the address, he offers to accompany you, still shocked into speechlessness, but you touch his shoulder, gently pat his hand and thank him.

He has done enough for you, a mere interpreter of English addresses.

For the second time in twenty-four hours, you are touched by Sandhya's childlike love for you. When she weeps, she forgets her usual beauty-queen posturing, blowing her nose into her *pallu*. You clutch her like you clutched your mother when you were leaving Wada.

Almost as if in a depressing De Chirico painting, you stare at a sight you haven't seen in the six years of your stay at Maska Chawl. What omen is this? You stare at the singing sensation, the drunk Time Office manager, lurching down the lane. He drowned your cry of pain and ecstasy the first night you made love.

It's almost dawn, but his ditty heralds the longest night in your life.

Sanjay pays the Sikh cab driver a large sum in advance, his last resolute act against *Nana*'s abuse. The old Sardar*ji* sees your battered face from the corner of his eye, plucks the trunk out of your hands and places it gently on the front seat, as if it holds a heart made of glass.

Thankfully for you, a dishevelled but genuinely worried Pankaj is waiting at the gate of his Marine Drive building. You've never been in a lift before, so you clutch his arm when he slams its sliding doors and it judders up the floors.

Your voice is hoarse. Your mind is blank. Your shoulder has an ugly welt. Your ribs hurt, but you clutch Sharan as if your life depends on him.

'Just let me stay for a day, for Sharan's sake, okay, then I will find...'

Find what, Mrs Patil?

Your question terrorises you.

Pankaj places a finger on his lips, 'Don't worry about anything now...just rest.'

Your new room has an old cupboard, a huge bed, and a dressing table, all a deep brown.

Pankaj insists that you clean your wounds with antiseptic, and you accede to his request, although all you want is to lie down and die.

❧ 16 ❧

The Night is Darkest

YOU WAKE UP MANY YEARS later to *Mai*'s voice, gurgling happily as a child lets out screams of delight.

'She is dead, *Mai*, how can she be here now?'

You prop yourself on your right elbow, use your left hand to push back the red-hot spikes protruding from the left of your head. There's bright light in the adjoining room. Sharan zooms closer, then recedes on the arcs of his screeches. Someone has not only made friends with Sharan, they have even created a makeshift swing for him at your bedroom door.

A woman squeezes past Sharan, carefully balancing a cup of tea, with a couple of glucose biscuits on the saucer. Grey hair, a million lines on the face, a toothless grin, nine-yard sari, but straight as a headmistress.

You sit up, disorientated. *Mai* is dead. This is not *Mai*.

The swing stops mid-air and you see a squeaky-clean tie-and-jacket-clad Pankaj picking Sharan off it.

'Maya*didi*, this is *Maavshi*. I told you about her when we met at the library. She has been staying with our family since I was a baby.' He speaks like an employer reeling off the credentials of a new employee.

'She looked after my mother for two years before her death. When my father migrated to Belgium for the diamond trade, he left her behind to look after me. I call her *Maavshi*...because I have never asked her her real name.' *Maavshi* lets out her patented gurgle, while she feigns to slap Pankaj's bottom. In his own house, Pankaj is able to shrug off and hang up his hesitancy like a robe. His actions become precise, like those of the diamond-cutters he hires.

He asks *Maavshi* to fill hot water for your bath, while he escorts you on a tour.

The house (Flat 5B, Hari Niwas, 77, Marine Drive) is huge, with as many as three bedrooms, and amazingly enough, each has a bathroom attached to it. The tub and the shower fascinate you. The balcony faces the sea in the West. The city rushes around on the arterial road below, oblivious to the storm in Girangaon that has washed up this new jetsam onto the beaches of Hari Niwas. You blink at the sea, inhale deep the sharp air, devoid of the cloying damp cloth smell, then touch your ribs in pain.

'Shall I rub some oil on your body?' *Maavshi* offers to alleviate your physical discomfort, but your head shakes a hasty 'No!' Not even Ravindra has seen you naked in daylight. Pankaj wants you to dress up and accompany him to his family doctor, to check your injuries.

When you enter the bathroom to get ready, it provides other surprises. You improvise by squatting on your feet on the edges of the commode. You use the water from the bucket, instead of the shower.

Sharan loves the sea of water in the bathtub. He insists on creating waves, so you finally allow him to stay in the tub with *Maavshi* keeping an eye on his underwater escapades.

The doctor insists on sending you to a clinic in Colaba, where you stand, holding your breath, for the X-ray.

Thankfully, that evening, the X-rays that Pankaj brings on his way back from his office show no lasting damage. Your bones, hardened perhaps by your mother's cooking and father's singing, have withstood the onslaught of an inebriated broom.

You both watch the sun melt into the Arabian Sea, Pankaj with Sharan in his lap, you with emotions so mixed, your mind tires of them. You admire Pankaj's patience with your silence. The traffic grows silent, Sharan nods off, and you realise that Pankaj has been drinking steadily.

You are too exhausted to sleep.

When you turn to him, he looks away, slurs, mumbles to himself, 'Without this, Maya, I would not have the courage to face the night...every night... it started with Krishna*rao*'s nightmares...this kills the pain.'

You are now worried that he may have misunderstood your rather prompt arrival after his invitation at the library. You begin to explain how very shortly you will find a home for yourself, and how grateful you are for his hospitality.

He is genuinely hurt.

'I live alone here, Maya*didi*, what is the big deal if I share it with someone I respect? I told you how similar our conditions are. Please, please, feel free to stay as long as you want... *Maavshi* knows everything about me, including the fact that I like Varun more than any girl...so she wouldn't mind...and she loves children...she once asked me to adopt a child...'

❧ 17 ❧
A Weary Mind Discovers its Own Truth

YOU SINK INTO A PRUSSIAN BLUE depression.

That leads to the first long illness of your life. Losing your appetite, you nurse a low-grade fever and find it difficult to wake up at your usual time at dawn. Despite the senses enjoying both the luscious expansiveness and the cotton wool intimacy of this new snuggery, your mind curls up into itself.

Pankaj's family doctor suggests a rest. Pankaj wonders if you should all go to the hills. You say you are too tired to make the effort.

Sharan senses the change but he has discovered a new universe of books that Pankaj has bought, a new house with spaces that allow him to run, a new grandmother who sings the same songs as the old.

While you wage your battles against your own mind, the nation has been forced into a war with China, and lost it. The naïve Prime Minister of a naïve, adolescent nation has committed what is called a 'Himalayan blunder'. For the first time, the nation realises what it is to be independent, to suffer the results of its actions.

In time, you too will have to do the same.

You convalesce by feasting on large, cool slabs of afternoon silence. You remember a strange crabby device that *Anna*, the village barber, used to trim your brother's hair, a nuchal lawn mower. That device chews through the fabric of your dreams, tearing the muslin between consciousness and deep sleep. You later realise it's merely the sound of the bell announcing the maid's arrival at the neighbour's that does this.

You sit staring at the sea, and drift out towards the horizon. Almost like a reflex action, you begin humming the *shloka* your father chanted for you.

Ripley's *Believe It or Not.* Astonishing but true. That is the only relationship from your past still intact!

Your relationship with a song.

What did it mean, really? What did your father want you to understand?

Pankaj feels guilty about your wan smiles. He attempts to get you interested in his collection of Western classical music. For his sake, you listen to the tinkle and the roar of Mozart and Beethoven. Perhaps subconsciously, your ear is much more seduced by modal music, not by continuously changing chord structures. You hear, but do not listen.

You are weighed down by your own listlessness.

The first incident that snaps you out of the slough of despondency is the discovery of Sharan getting totally absorbed by the music. Somewhere, on those millions of chromosome sites that he has inherited from you, must be sketched the prescription for what psychologists refer to as musical intelligence. The oddest part of his addiction is his manner of listening to the music. He sits still, not necessarily erect, but staring into nothingness. The records become his most prized new toys. He abandons his books, forcing *Maavshi* to play the records endlessly.

The next Saturday, Pankaj brings home a surprise guest.

Varun, the poet's son.

Varun touches your shoulder gingerly, eager to express his empathy, yet unsure of his gestures.

Three victims gagged by circumstance.

'How's...your father?' you ask, polite despite yourself. 'He's busy...been invited to Russia, there is an International Workers' Poetry Seminar...'

Pankaj proposes a party. You are not very sure how to respond. He senses your hesitation.

'Let's at least go and watch a movie.'

You go to Strand, a theatre in Colaba that screens Hollywood hits. In the darkness, you notice Varun and Pankaj holding hands. The movie is a thriller, and Sharan expresses his dislike of the noise, so you walk out and sit with him in the lobby.

Dinner is at the Taj Hotel. There are no marble statues rinsing hair in waterfalls of light, like at Copper Chimney, where you discovered your motherhood and Ravindra discovered his doubts. There are foreigners instead. You are terrified. The increased number of forks and spoons do not make the experience any more pleasant. You are glad to return to your new home. Varun stays over, since anyway Krishna*rao* is not in town and no explanations for his absence are needed.

One particular evening, still immersed in your depression, you are reminded of the experiments at Esalen, the institute your father mentioned. You put off the lights in the bathroom. Then you slip into the tub until your ears are under water.

The eyes see blackness, the ears hear the giant susurration of breath, the skin feels wombwater, the tongue tastes nothing, the nose smells the lavender in the bubble bath.

Then deep inside your mind, a question raises its hood.

'Who are you?'

A bubble detonates near your ear.

You regress to the river, to your brother, to your father. Relive memories you never knew existed.

You are swinging under the gossamer shadows of tiny leaves.

Light, shade, light, shade.

You are in deep sleep, yet are able to hear someone sobbing. A big hand picks up your palm, holds it against his chest.

Dada, before you left the village?

Krishna*rao*, in your sea-lullaby sleep?

Ravindra, asking his heart, wrestling his doubt about his gonads and your womb?

'Who are you?'

A waterdrop plops, distilling meaning in the silence.

'Who are you?'

You were *Baba*'s goddess, you were *Dada*'s doll, you were your mother's accomplice, you were, maybe, Ravindra's muse...but *before*, and *after*, and *besides*, and *outside* of relationships, who are you?

'Nobody.'

'When I am not worrying about my father leaving, my mother leaving, my *Dada* leaving, my husband leaving...I...am...nobody.'

The steam scrubs off the stubborn stains on your mind.

'Who are you?'

'*Chidanandarupah*', answers a hoarse voice.

It is your father's voice, his last urgent message of survival for you.

Silence.

You hear the air rubbing against the cartilage of your windpipe, sandpapering it into smoothness. You hear your breath, your body's umbilical cord of oxygen, binding you to the universe, to mottled Jupiter choked with dust, to the Ganges dolphin washed up on unknown clay, to a Greenland snowflake showing off its fractal edges.

You are back into a river seventeen years ago. But this time you know what is happening.

Inside you, two depths merge.

One is the meaning of the *shloka*, the meaning beyond words.

The other is the long series of those moments since childhood, when your sense of your self dissolved into rain and dusk and breath and infinity.

In one explosive moment, the two merge.

You are pure awareness and eternal bliss.

Everything else is illusion, Maya.

Everything else is illusion, like your name.

Yes. Yes. Yes.

That's what it means. That's what your father wanted you to understand. Don't worry about the name of the relationship and what it implies. You are neither daughter nor wife nor mother nor sister nor friend nor goddess.

You are pure awareness and eternal bliss. Begin from there, relate from there.

You smile in the darkness. You have returned from the

lip of an abyss. You have decided to walk by yourself towards the home of light.

You will live up to an innocent promise made to your father. You will learn not to depend on anybody.

When you step out of the tub, you step out of your muddy old skin, display a translucent body.

When the three men in your life sit at the table the next morning, and you and *Maavshi* serve breakfast, you enjoy the ceremony attached to it, since you have never imagined breakfast as a meal deserving so much attention.

Suddenly, there appears to be no darkness surrounding your lives. Your heart soars with the pigeon flocks when they take off at Marine Drive.

When you actually start playing hide and seek with him in the house, Sharan realises you are back with him.

The young girls and boys at the library welcome you with a box of *pedas*, bought through a collective contribution. At the end of the month, you hand over the 200 rupees to Pankaj; you don't want to depend on anybody.

He hands it back over to you, mumbling, 'It's okay, I'm not doing charity, I owe you much more than you understand...you are the first human being I know after *Maavshi* who makes me feel whole and clean...you've turned this house into a home...don't worry, if you become a burden, I'll tell you...'

But you will no longer take 'No' for an answer. You hand over the money to *Maavshi* to use for home expenses.

You decide you will find a better job, a way of living where nobody has rights over where you are, what you do.

But before you embark on your refugee trail once

again, you will make one last concession to yourself and suck dry the fleshy fruits of hedonism.

You will taste freedom.

You slice the day into clean sections. You roll in your bed in the early mornings, choosing to paint the interstices between those moments with opaque cadmium. You luxuriate in a synaesthetic sea, the latent fire of the yellow infiltrated by a happy languor to the precise chromatic tension. Your body sings under the satin sheets, you never knew you could drown depression in two-and-a-half inches of skin. Sometimes you remember Ravindra and squeeze your nipples under the coarse cotton blouse, tweak them, like a guitarist squeezing his keys just so that the cadmium yellow is squeezed under your eyelids and flows out in warm tears.

You sigh in naked pleasure.

Late mornings are time for a *memsaahib*'s bath. Wrapped in an old bathing gown, you run hot water into the tub, splash the ancient bubble bath salts.

'Never been in a bathtub before, *haan*?' Pankaj smiles indulgently one Saturday, when he witnesses your elaborate ritual. 'Never been naked for a bath before in my entire life, Pankaj,' you want to explain as you shut the door, causing the bathroom to darken.

The slower you perform the ceremonial immersion, the better it feels. You slip out of your sari, your undergarments. The petticoat strings have left behind their souvenir on the skin around your waistline. You'd never realised it yourself until now that your body had forgotten nakedness. The fifth sense had put down its shutters at puberty. Still spread over twenty square feet of skin, it can pass on a lot of information. As you feel your calves, your thighs ('Snake tongues lick, Smooth white pith of your thighs, Lick the fruit of a million sighs'), your breasts, the first integument of Brahman sighs in pleasure.

'*Na cha shrotrajivhe na cha ghraananetre...*'

'I am neither voice nor taste, neither smell nor sight...'

With *Maavshi*'s help, you decide to show Varun, Pankaj and Sharan what a real festival of light is, since Diwali is round the corner.

It's time you did something for Pankaj for all the help he has displayed.

You spend time with *Maavshi* in the kitchen, picking and choosing, frying the *besan*, squeezing the *chakalis* out of the star-shaped anus of the *chakali*-maker, patting the *laddoos* into shape, rolling the little brass wheels to create fluted edges of *karanjis*.

Sharan is endlessly fascinated by this process.

When you squat on the floor to work at the complex preparations he stands with one hand on your shoulder, one on his hips, one leg bent locked behind the other, like Lord Krishna, staring at the fine lace of tiny bubbles that magically appears when flour meets 180°C oil, at *karanjis* growing brown and bloat-bellied even before you can flip them over, at *laddoos* getting dimpled by their own weight.

On the morning of the first day of Diwali, you make Sharan and Pankaj go through the ritual of a four-stage bath. Cool air seeps through the cracks in the dawn sky. Warm unguents and potions are rubbed on to their hairless bodies and into their hair. The air explodes with the heavy fragrances of sandalwood and camphor. After a steaming hot bath, both are instructed to stand outside the house at the threshold, crush the demon of a bitter fruit under their big toes and taste its green blood. You laugh till there are tears in your eyes while a sloping-shouldered, *dhoti*-wearing Sharan chases his slippery demon.

Then they enter the house, conquistadors, sultans, masters of the universe, banishers of darkness, harbingers of light, metaphorical sons of Lord Ram, the ideal male. They are worshipped with light and love, made to sit on intricately carved wooden seats and served the snacks you have so meticulously created for them. The day ends with Sharan lighting rockets that zoop and fizz into the sky at Marine Drive.

As you watch his fascination at this magical happening, your heart is cleansed of all ashes.

☙ 18 ❧
What a Party

PANKAJ'S PARTY MATERIALISES on a Saturday in the dry coolness of a January evening. You have asked Pankaj's permission and phoned Sandhya and Sanjay at Goverdhan*Bhai*'s. The two of them walk in shyly, but are put at ease by *Maavshi*. You hug Sandhya, you don't know the name of your relationship, but you owe her so much. You hug Sanjay too, now unafraid of how the gesture will be interpreted.

Besides Varun, there is Sylvia, who works as a secretary in Pankaj's office, Mr Ganguly, family-friend and tax consultant, a handsome young employee of Pankaj's called Mahadevan, and Mrs Shah, a diamond merchant's wife. Mrs Shah, a cultural oddity who is aware of her unique status, has a keen interest in literature, English as well as Marathi. Her thin eyebrows sit very high above her eyes, giving her the look of a permanently startled rabbit.

She talks about Sandwana emeralds from the Rio Tinto mines, *tussore* from the Begum family of Chittagong, Dylan Thomas's *Under Milkwood* and Krishna*rao*'s songs.

'I love pure sound,' she purrs.

She flings exotic words like pearls before you swine: Cuspidor (apparently James Joyce's favourite), euphonium, jonquil, bobolink. They float to the carpet, shatter on impact, sublimate and release tendrils of patchouli and lavender. She corners Varun and explains to him why she likes his father's, Krishna*rao*'s, poetry: because he impregnates Marathi words, weighs them down with brocade and *zari*.

These remarks freeze up the air between the two, but she hardly notices.

For a tax consultant, Mr Ganguly appears very soft and gentle. You notice his duck-tailed nape hair as he plays with Sharan. 'Sharan, beautiful name, Mrs Patil, only Bengalis and Maharashtrians try to give meaningful names, otherwise see this South Indian... Mahadevan! Why are you not wearing the river Ganga in your head, Mahadevan?' Mahadevan laughs, obviously this remark has been exchanged before. Instead of the river Ganga, Mahadevan walks around dragging a faint cloud of sandalwood perfume over his head. Sylvia's amber eyes twinkle, as the gin takes effect. You refuse to drink, remembering the explosion in your gut the beer once triggered.

As the evening proceeds, Pankaj announces that Sylvia is going to sing. She has a husky voice, smoke plus sunshine-on-hay plus nostalgia. '...*but whatever your dreams may be, dream a little dream of me*...' You have never heard the song before, yet the voice seems to affect you more than everybody else, reminding you of other voices, and their owners.

You are still dreaming of Ravindra. The memories of your togetherness are far stronger than the memories of his letter.

The crystalline silence, a moment after the song finishes, is broken not by applause, but by the harsh *trrraaannng* of the doorbell. *Maavshi* answers the door, and somehow everybody senses her discomfiture.

Finally she just leaves the door open and whispers your name.

It is Ravindra.

The light above the lintel bathes his forehead and his wonderful cheekbones, so you recognise him even though he has grown a beard, hiding the pockmarks.

Ravindra.

He showed you what lay under the quilted skirts of mountains. He demonstrated how to use the Morse code of colour instead of words. He slapped awake the slumbering anaconda of desire between your thighs.

Ravindra.

You rush towards him and hug him. He smells of an alien woody perfume, yet your nostrils hunt out his acid sweat smell. He too holds you wordlessly, sniffling. You don't remember how long you stand there.

There are awkward introductions, then Ravindra notices Sanjay, and Pankaj. Pankaj offers a way to end the stalemate.

'Why don't you take him to your room, Maya?'

The door shuts. Husband and wife face each other with new faces.

Ravindra smiles when he sees Sharan sleeping on the bed in your room. He sits by his side, hesitates, touches his tiny palm. Sharan's fingers curl around his stained finger.

Many years ago, your fingers had curled around a rough finger too.

You try to hold Ravindra's other palm, but he pulls his

hand away, distracted. He explains that he could not come to India after *Mai*'s death. Flight tickets were impossible, and he had given up. He had returned to Maska Chawl at the end of his scholarship period yesterday, and came to know all that had happened from the neighbours.

'Come let's go back home,' he says, picking up Sharan, laying him on his left shoulder. You stand at the door leading to the balcony, your back to the West, your face to the East, on the threshold of your new life.

He notices your pause. He smiles reassuringly, but his voice smells of barely controlled anger. 'Come on, Maya, I'm here now, everything will be all right...let's not make an exhibition of ourselves before strangers.'

You stand at a threshold.

'Maya, *Nana* hurt you...but what did I do wrong?'

Your silence hurts him.

Ravindra waits, tightens his jaws, takes a deep breath before he continues. 'Look. Where will he go? Old man...don't you understand...under stress of *Mai*'s going away...' his voice drops towards the end.

It is time for you to stop lying to him.

You whisper, not wanting to hurt him, not wanting to suffer metal tearing your blouse again, 'I read your letter to *Mai* and *Nana*.'

The eighteen months in Paris are too short to have acquired the Frenchman's famed *sang-froid*. The muscles of his face no longer obey his mind.

'So?' he snarls, comes closer. The pockmarks bunch up under the new beard.

'You believe I committed a sin...you do not trust me...'

Your heart quietens. You have made the final leap

across the chasm.

'How can I?' he screams. Sharan turns uncomfortably in his arms.

'The moment you found Sanjay you ran away from me, the moment you found the poet you ran away from Sanjay, the moment you meet this bloody Pankaj, you run away...! Right now, you are enjoying a party while your father-in-law sleeps hungry in his own home, I can't believe this...he, I, we brought you to this city from that dirty little village...you little shit...'

You seem to be on the threshold for an eternity. The angrier Ravindra gets, the surer you feel about your decision.

'...and you are such a proud bitch you will refuse to live with your husband, a man whose *mangalsutra* you wear still...you do not bother what people will say about you...your own brother...your father-in-law...'

He raises his hand to hit you, stops when he sees the silence in your eyes.

The name of the relationship is husband-wife. But hiding under its eternally smiling mask is mistrust and anger and fear.

You have made your choice about this charade long before this night.

Unfortunately, Ravindra has been unable to make his choices. He does not know what to do about his own father, his own wife, his own unproven suspicions.

The French funambulist.

He freezes when you walk up to him, extract Sharan out of his limp arms and lay him back on the bed. You *shush* Sharan till his breathing is even.

Then you get up, walk up to Ravindra, touch his

pockmarked face, 'Look, Sharan is your son... I don't care what your father believes, my brother believes...'

'Then come home...' he screams.

'Not until you say you believe me...'

He falls silent, breathing hard.

You whisper, wanting him to carry his journey to its logical end, 'Look...I...I have nothing...not even your trust...you were born with something very few human beings have...it's the one thing that can never leave you...it is proven...the world says so...it will give the fame you want...but I am going to try and find what I want out of life...'

'Shut up, you *putain*, you *raand*, don't tell me what to do... I know what you want...you just want the world to believe that I am not a man,' he boils over, resorting to French and mill-town filth to utter the one obscenity he has held back.

Sharan lets out a wail in his sleep. The door handle turns. Two hesitant heads pop in.

'You okay?' Varun and Pankaj ask together.

Ravindra rushes out, shouldering aside the door and Pankaj and Varun. You pick up Sharan, clutch him closer, *shush* him again, inhale that intoxicating smell of the top of his head.

No more crying. No more. 'Neither will I cry, nor will I give you reason to do so.'

The night grows as cool as a knife.

Once Sharan goes back to sleep, you come out into the silence of the house, wanting to be held by *Maavshi*.

To your astonishment, the others are still around, silently gulping their dinner.

Why are they there? Haven't they had their fill of a

hideous spectacle? Haven't Sanjay and Sandhya heard you being called a whore once before? You rush to the kitchen, where *Maavshi* clutches your arm and whispers, 'He left of his own accord, my child, don't carry his burden with you.'

You hug her while she keeps whispering, 'Don't, don't worry my *sona*, better times will return.'

Despite your tense face, Pankaj drags you out by your hand, and his next announcement surprises you. 'Friends, I'm sorry about what happened to my sister, my friend, my confidante today. But we have come here not to commiserate, but celebrate. Maya comes from a village where the birthdays of grown-ups are not celebrated. Unfortunately for her, in this house, there is no escape. So let's show her how we do it!'

They all break into a 'Happy birthday to you' song. Your head is in a tizzy. You are twenty-seven, homeless, husbandless, fatherless, motherless, with a job that will not pay for your son's future, and you are being asked to celebrate your birthday. Mahadevan kisses you on the cheek and then kisses Sylvia on her lips, Mr Ganguly hugs you gently, Pankaj hugs *Maavshi* as if his life depends on her, but you hear snatches of the conversation, 'She is exactly like Aditi*didi*, *Maavshi*, exactly.'

Now, instead of asking Sylvia to sing, Pankaj uses his LP records. That is a cue for Mahadevan and Sylvia to start dancing, and even the ever-startled rabbit, Mrs Shah, with the gin inside her, is turning nifty pirouettes around Mr Ganguly.

You realise you have actually had several gulps of beer from Pankaj's glass. Swallowing the bitter drink feels like good revenge against your husband's anger. In the following haze, you remember being forced to dance. You have danced before, but those were circular rhythms, young girls dancing with each other the dances of innocence, celebrating a good harvest, celebrating the beginning of spring, celebrating the return to the cocoon of their mothers' homes after marriage.

Instead, these are mating dances, hands touching forbidden parts of the body, the lower back, front of thighs against thighs, the brush against breasts ('Sorry,' says Pankaj), warm finger tips on the soft inside of your upper arm.

Thankfully, you feel safe with Pankaj. You have never laughed so much, even screamed so much. You drag Sanjay and Sandhya on to the floor, join hands and dance a threesome dance that has no name or form, it is a private celebration of three people wanting to protect the only purity they know in their lives.

The past is a whirl of illusion, it was a dream, when you stop twirling around, you will wake up, and the reality of your life will regain equilibrium.

Thank god for the teak solid doors of Hari Niwas. Sharan sleeps through it all. When you finally slide into sleep next to Sharan in the wee hours of the morning, you wonder at the distance you have travelled from your village.

You hope you are free from everything it stood for.

✌ 19 ✍

A Universe of Questions

SHARAN'S RELATIONSHIP WITH music seems to have awakened his sense of speech. *Mai* used to say he was a quiet child, but had she been around now she would have changed her opinion rather quickly.

As you go about your chores, he follows you, punctuating every task with a question. Some of the answers you speak aloud, the others can only echo inside the chambers of your loneliness.

'*Aai*, when the water in the tub goes down where does it go?'

'Back into the sea, I think.'

'Then does the sea overflow?'

'No, because somebody else is also using the water. From the sea (remember your teacher in Wada asking you geography questions?) it evaporates...'

'Evaporates...what does it mean...?'

'It becomes clouds and then becomes rain and then becomes, what? An eternal symbol of separation. Will I be ever separated from you? Will there be rain at that moment?'

'*Aai*, is this your house or Pankaj *maamaa's* house?'

'It is Pankaj *maamaa's* house...and every time you ask this question I get angry with myself. I promise you, we will have a house of our own. You and me. Inseparable.'

'*Aai*, *Maavshi* says she was born in a village. What is a village?'

'It has farms and cattle (Shankar, unafraid of rivers in spate) and cacti and mud roads and rivers and...Brahmins who everybody is scared of except a girl crazed by the love of her brother...also her father...'

'*Aai*, Pankaj *maamaa* says he had a sister who went away without telling him. Do I have a sister? Do I have a brother? Do you have a sister? Do you have a brother?'

'No you have no sisters or brothers...I have, I had...I had a brother whom I loved and who died and I have a brother who is alive and whom I refuse to keep in touch with for no fault of his...can't you ask anything else?'

'*Aai*, do you like the music I like?'

'I don't know. If you like it, it's okay for me. I will do whatever it takes for you to pursue what you like.'

It's a stupid promise to make. It will make you wander in a wasteland of loneliness for twelve long years.

'Aai, are you afraid of the dark, like I am?'

'No. Yes. Depends on which dark. There is the dark of night where a face sprang up, lit by glow-worms. I am not afraid of that dark. But there is a dark that laughs at me. It says I don't have the wherewithal to look after you by myself. That dark is a wall. I can't push it away. I will gather strength to fight it, but I don't know, I don't know.'

'*Aai*, why did *Baba* leave?'

'Because...because the answer is too complicated and you should not be given the answer right now. Go to sleep.'

'*Aai, Mai-ajji* used to pray to god. Who is he?'

'Don't know. Sometimes she's a hungry monster who eats up brothers. Sometimes a benign guy who answers prayers of artists who want a scholarship. Now go to sleep.'

Why do children ask questions that pierce as swiftly as poison-tipped arrows?

❦ 20 ❦
The Long March Home

THE LIBRARY becomes your anchor for the next few years.

That one evening in suspended darkness in the tub seems to have provided a centripetal force that swallows the storms within you. You are happier still that Pankaj is now accepting the money you earn: however little, it makes you feel less like a refugee and more like a member of a family.

You have so much spare time, you start maintaining a diary. You write down memories, angry and sad poems, letters to your father. You attempt to translate what you like in Marathi into English and vice versa.

The youngsters in the library notice one small change: you have begun reading the newspapers in earnest too. What are you looking for? Certainly not news on the next Sammelan? You laugh at the student who makes that remark. You have had your fill of Sammelans.

The last one is just a fading semicolon in the song you now want to sing.

The truth is, you don't know what kind of a job you

are looking for.

One afternoon, you even walk down to the Metro cinema across the railway tracks, and enrol yourself as a jobless youth in the State Government Employment Bureau. It is while filling their form that you discover the peculiarity of your position: You might believe you are well-read, even others might, but you are not *formally* educated.

You have no school certificates, no college degrees, no proof. What do you write against the legend 'Education'? 'Can quote from "Songs of the Madder Soil", loves whatever she has read of Anaïs Nin, learnt her first lessons about separation and sadness at the age of twelve?'

'We don't see things as they are, we see them as we are,' Ms Nin had said.

You write to schools out of Bombay, for a job as a nursery or primary school teacher, to big libraries in small towns, to care centres for paraplegics and the elderly. Most of your letters are returned with no response.

You then consider a job as a correspondent or a regular feature writer.

When Mr Mhatre from *Navin Mahila* drops in the next time, you ask him if such a career is possible, and how much it would pay. The sum he mentions appears inadequate to stay in a place of your own, look after Sharan's education, be independent.

One impatient morning, you ask *Maavshi* if as a last resort you should start selling home-made snacks. After all, you are good at making them, aren't you? *Maavshi* sees a difference between being independent and living alone. She maintains that in society, it is difficult for a woman to be alone. Anyway, you are not living off anybody, you are paying for your food and shelter.

At the end of eight months of searching for a job, you catch yourself scratching around like an irritated hen, getting short-tempered even with Sharan.

When you sit, penitent, staring at the sea, you see where this river has started its poisonous journey.

For the first time in your life, you have pursued something, rather than flow with the tide. QED, dear Maya, remember the classical definition of emotion: the response of the mind to blockage of aims?

You hug and kiss Sharan, and blow *parping* bugle sounds against his tight soft tummy, and when he gurgles helplessly, you become whole again.

When it does arrive, the opportunity for independence is a simple 15-paise inland letter from a residential school in Mahabaleshwar. It smells of black soil, ragged temperatures and hope. 'We received your application, and while impressed by the fact that you are well-read, we are bound by the laws of the land to appoint teachers of only a minimum state-recognised qualification. Hence we must reject your application.'

'However,' it continues a tiny somersault of your heart later, 'we are eager to fill the post of a housemistress, who by definition is a foster mother to the children who live in a hostel. We need a housemistress for a hostel of twenty young boys and girls, and one of our attractive perks is free education for your son, Sharan. Your "qualification" as a mother seems appropriate for this job. Needless to add, the campus is beautiful, and the salary, though not very high, can lead to a lot of savings since boarding and lodging is paid for. Should you be interested...' The rest of the letter is difficult to read because your eyes are brimming with tears of happiness.

You kiss the letter and draft a reply.

Two weeks later, the school has sent you their acceptance: they will pay for your bus trip, and if you like what you see, you can stay there or return to Bombay for your baggage. Pankaj and *Maavshi* don't know how to react. Sharan and you have filled an empty house with laughter, colour and noise. Pankaj's response is a farewell party. This time, the mood is sombre. You are touched by the fact that each one has brought a gift for you or Sharan. Mrs Shah gives you a rare Tibetan ring to ward off all evil, Mr Ganguly has got books for about-to-be-five-year-olds, Sylvia and Mahadevan have got books for you on Education (*Why Children Fail* and *The Montessori Method*).

You insist on Sylvia singing her song once again after so many years: '...*but whatever your dreams may be, dream a little dream of me*...'

Who do you want to dream of you? Ravindra? Pankaj? Or Sharan?

At midnight, after everybody has left, you sit with Pankaj in the balcony. There is some light pre-monsoon April rain. The street lamp is level with the balcony, and in its light, the rain is a shower of mercury droplets that do not reach the road below.

Rain, the eternal witness of every milestone in your life.

At the cost of being insensitive to all Pankaj has done, you hold his hand, kiss it and tell him how it is not possible for you to express your gratitude. You respect him even more for not struggling to give your relationship a name. For four long years, he has provided you with an anchor in a drifting world. He hugs you until you are out of breath. 'No, he should not drive you up to Mahabaleshwar. Yes, you will be okay using the State Transport bus. No, you do not know exactly where this school is. Yes, the directions to the school are very clear.'

The horizontal iron bars of the bus window play their usual role of separating the past and the future. You sit there at your seat, truth be told, a trifle excited. This is the first time in your life you have decided to leave others and walk away with a clear purpose. *Maavshi* has created a record: she has stepped out of Hari Niwas for the second time in the years after the departure of Pankaj's parents.

Surrounded by the stench of diesel, stale sugarcane juice, sweaty hawkers and unwashed vomit on the side of the bus, *Maavshi* musters enough courage to reveal her heart, at an uncommon place and time. Just like your husband did even before his juices had dried between your thighs.

'I never got to see my children grow, my *sona*, I am sure you will. You have the strength of a man and the strength of a woman...both...go my child.'

Then she covers her lips with her *pallu* to hide her weeping.

Pankaj just stares at you.

Yes, that other brother too touched you last through the horizontal bars of a bus window.

❧ 21 ❧
Return to Paradise

YOU OPEN THE GIANT GATES of 'New Era: The Best Co-educational, Residential School in the Sahyadris', expecting to be accosted by a shout. Your entry obeys the classic rules of montage explained by Eisenstein: the image of the gate opening away from camera, drawing noisy scratches on a hyaline sky, juxtaposed against a close up of your eyes looking upwards, those deep black vaults that hide memory spools of twenty-seven years.

It's a Sunday, and the hairy hand of discipline that winds up the students like toys and lets them cover the stuttering distance from six at dawn to ten at night has relaxed.

Two hundred boys and girls from Classes One to Ten, five-years-old to fifteen, are busy scrubbing between their toes in the bathrooms, combing their cowlicks into place, masturbating over the young dance teacher's Annual Day photographs, neatly touching up the biology diagrams, cross sections of the *medulla oblongata* including *pons Varolii* and *thalamus*, snuffling in their adrenaline-engined fantasies, writing long letters to their mothers in newly-discovered cursive, arguing with the tuck shop owner, playing table tennis, all the *tock-tock tock-tock* cutting the thin Mahabaleshwar air, oblivious to your presence, your Eisenstein-directed entry into their cinema of unripe dreams.

The elderly *darwaan* carries your tin trunk, accompanying you to the Principal's house. Mrs Luthra, the Principal, is a huge woman with a delicate owl face, thick painted eyebrows, her pupils exaggerated into slippery black grapes by concave glasses. Her paw covers Sharan's face when she admires him. She speaks to you in Hindi, gesticulates towards the hostels, waddles breathlessly along with you to your guest cottage overlooking the valley.

On cue, a little girl in white skirts peeps from behind the babool bushes that protect the periphery with their hard thorns. She is sucking her thumb. Mrs Luthra explodes in joy. 'Manisha! You have been waiting for your *didi* right? Here she is! Will you show her the dining hall and the prayer hall, *beta*?'

You kneel down to receive your hostess. Manisha walks wordlessly up to you, and stops, stomach thrust ahead, shoulders sloping, eyes waiting to make a decision. 'Manisha is very clever,' continues Mrs Luthra, 'but rarely speaks.'

'That's not true,' you whisper suddenly to Manisha, 'she never speaks *because* she is clever.'

Manisha sacrifices the grip on the thumb for a moment, to grace you with a fleeting smile. You remember someone else who never spoke in school. So you resort to the language you know. You hug Manisha. 'We women know all the ancient languages, languages without scripts, languages without syllables.'

The next hour is a colour and fragrance banquet for your undernourished senses. Manisha holds one finger of one hand, Sharan of the other hand, and this six-legged creature wends its drunken way to the prayer hall of 'New Era, the Best Co-educational, Residential School in the Sahyadris'.

The prayer hall is situated at the edge of a plateau overlooking a magnificent valley. Three thousand feet below, veins of sparkling silver carry messages from the vaginas of rock down to the sea, many memories away. Patchwork quilts of green soak the sun, their bottoms moist, their tops toasty. The prayer hall contains a bubble of stillness on which floats a flat roof. The walls can barely cope with the quietude oozing out of its pores and the wind slamming it from the outside.

Manisha then leads you to the dining hall. The path is a corridor of fragrance: mango and *neem*, and a bunch of trees you can't identify because they are native to the plateau with the black soil. There is a pool of crushed red under a *gulmohar*, a pool of lavender under a jacaranda, a pool of pink under a bougainvillaea. Sharan is less tired and more hurt that he has to walk so much with you around. You pick him up, inhale the fragrance of his head, and the smell of *ameya*, the mango blossom, and deep inside, you are ecstatic.

'Please let me be alive, that's all I ask of you, my dear forgotten ancestors, shutter-eye gods, puissant spirits, cunning dryads, let me be alive to smell, see, touch, hear, taste...take away everything but leave intact my doorways to eternity.'

As usual, you do not suspect how seriously that entire bunch of supplication receivers will treat your request.

✿ 22 ✿
The Gilded Cage

YOUR NEW HOME is four rooms in the corner of the hostel where Manisha stays.

The back opens to a kitchen garden with a forest of papaya, banana, lime and laburnum. The front leads to a stone quadrangle, the playground for your twenty wards who have just finished their annual tests and are readying themselves to go home. Mrs Luthra's plan is an intelligent one: managing the departure of the children gives you an opportunity to meet the parents, and the holidays after give you enough time to understand the workings of the school.

For the first time in your life, you feel like laying out your territorial piss-marks in your home. Maybe because this is *your* home, not your father's or husband's or a new-found brother's. Adorning the corner table in the living room is Sandhya's beaded card to her loving elder sister, Mrs Shah's Tibetan ring, a thank you card from the kids at the library. You painstakingly write out your favourite chant on a sheet of handmade paper and stick it on the mirror.

The next morning, you attend your first assembly, and the school's last, for the term. Two hundred children in crisp white uniforms chant a *shloka* that sends a current of recognition up your spine.

'*Manobuddhi ahankaar chittaani naaham na cha...*'

It is chanted to a different rhythm, yet it cannot but carry in its troughs faint memories of a firefly-studded voice, a shower of *paarijaat* flowers. Mrs Luthra's owl eyes spot both Sharan and you mouthing the words, and she files away the fact in her prodigious memory vaults. The ebb and flow of the sound mimics the sea, and for a moment your senses are confused. The assembly ends with a resounding 'Aum'.

In the ensuing silence, you can feel the beginning of the universe.

It's time for introductions. Mrs Luthra explains how, if you, Mrs Patil, like what you see, you could well be that genuinely caring housemistress they have been looking for, for the youngest hostel, Laburnum House. The different teachers, Desai, Kunte, Pardiwalla, Premji, Kamath, and then you lose count, all greet you with polite '*Namastes*'. Though they seem a bit unsure of the pigeonhole of your marital status, Sharan, the *kumkum* and the *mangalsutra* provide a satisfactory bulwark against uncharitable conclusions.

The school brochure speaks about the true meaning of education, *educare*, *educe*, to lead out, to draw out the latent talent and potentiality of a child. For over twenty years, the New Era school has pursued this objective single-mindedly, in the process creating for the nation captains of industry, leaders of men, professionals with adamantine virtue and clear-eyed civic servants, those silent scriptwriters of a new India.

There is indeed a larger share of professionals among the school's patrons, unlike those *nouveau riche* schools with automatic washing machines and fancy horseriding classes, explains Mrs Sharma, a white sari-swaddled widow who looks after the older girls' hostel.

You want to tell her that in the first place, you had never heard of schools where students reside with teachers. Your idea of a school was four hours on a cotton *dhurrie* clutching a black slate, tongue repeating what the teacher sang and heart soaring with the kites in the sky.

Under instructions from Mrs Luthra, Mrs Sharma puts you through the paces: keeping account of the children's pocket money, of the laundry, of the tuck shop bills and overseeing the homework. For the first time in your life, you feel insecure. Have you bitten off more than you can chew?

You decide against returning to Bombay for the remaining four weeks of summer vacation. You must not fall short of anybody's expectations...not when this is your first opportunity to be yourself. You immerse yourself in a familiarisation drive: not just the hostel but also the labs, the offices, the tennis and basketball courts, the artificial lake, the amphitheatre. Sharan romps in the children's playground: when he screams and gurgles in pleasure on the swing, it reminds you of him on the swing after that dark night. This is a different universe, and it mellows you enough to write to Pankaj and *Maavshi*, inviting them to visit Sharan and you.

Some of the teachers, the bachelors, return to their hometowns in Bombay or Poona or Nasik, some with families go on a vacation, the older ones stay on campus. You make friends with the childless Mr and Mrs Naik, he a maths teacher, she a geography teacher, also doubling up as the housemistress of Gulmohar House, the hostel where the older girls reside; with Mr Bhatkhande, the music teacher who lives with his shy seventeen-year-old daughter, Kausalya; with Khot, the peon who has travelled all the way from Konkan; and with Bhivaji, father of the gardens, greenthumb, interpreter of the black soil's cravings.

You tell Bhivaji how as a child you thought you could hear the xylem sucking water from the red soil and he breaks into a toothless grin. Yes, you understand the secret life of plants. He tells you how the trees mourn for their siblings, shed leaves in anger or grow faster when he hugs them on cold nights. He opens a creaky door to the unsullied paradise you experienced in Wada. You wander endlessly with him and Sharan, while he talks about each tree as if it were his child.

When he realises that you are reading out the botanical names from your old handbook of *Flora and Fauna in Western India,* he hatches a plan to create name-plates for his favourite trees. Imagine, when the children return, they will know his trees by both their Indian and English names. It's a delightful plan. It keeps you occupied for days on end. Mr Bhatkhande and you get Mrs Luthra's permission, and before you know it, with Kausalya's help, you have added at least fifty new recognisable residents to the campus.

The ectomorphic *ashoka* trees, sentinels on parade, the jacarandas, powder blue Brazilian imports, the intoxicating *kadamba,* favourite of Lord Krishna, the outwardly hardy *neem*, weeping silent sap tears. Their knees now carry their first names and family names, ending their refugee status.

You remember one magical full moon night, sitting outside the prayer hall, your back against a *gulmohar*'s thigh, watching the river snake slough off its silver skin. Mr Bhatkhande and Kausalya are practising classical singing together, and Sharan lies hypnotised in your arms.

It is not just water that flows through rivers. Sound flows, blood flows, time flows.

If ever an etching could be liquid, then a river is an etching of time.

๛ 23 ๛
6000mm

THE TEACHERS RETURN a week before the arrival of the students to manage the process of new admissions. You are impressed by the earnestness of the parents who accompany the youngsters. Have you thought enough about Sharan's education? Provisions for his future? Insurance for his illness? You admit you have not, and you slip into a pensive mood.

Since the students have not yet arrived, the dinners at the dining hall become exuberant, loud get-togethers for the staff. Stories are exchanged with much backslapping, the bachelors whisper saucy jokes to each other and guffaw, the older couples smile and share their own secrets. Consumption of alcohol on the campus, though not banned by policy, is frowned upon, but your Krishna*rao* and *Nana*-trained nose informs you that some of the bachelors indulge.

During one of these sessions, Mrs Luthra lets it out that it was you who thought of naming the trees, and Kausalya, who likes to mix with the younger teachers, mentions that your criticism of a famous poet was once published. A couple of teachers remember the fracas around the Sammelan, but it is too distant a memory to be interesting.

Somehow this new angle to your profile immediately grants you a passport into at least one inner circle. Ulka and Urmi, the twins who teach Marathi as an optional subject in a school whose medium of instruction is English, insist on a monsoon session for the Marathi caucus at your hostel. Over the years you will understand that all the caucuses are hopelessly intertwined, the school is an island cut off from the rest of the universe, obsessed by its past.

3,530 feet above sea level, rain discards its gentility. Not for it the artful slant that kisses the lower plains. Here it is a shameless wall of water. Inside three months, it will unload six thousand millimetres.

Unfortunately, the lone blue inland letter lying in your letterbox smells of the other rain. Even before you reach your room, mop your head and face with your *pallu*, and meaninglessly adjust your *bindi*, you know in your bones that the rain is merely a reminder of the antics of fate.

'Dear Maya,
I thought you would return with me when I came to you last. Instead you run further away.
Perhaps we should legalise our divorce. I know I will be laughed at, but I have already been laughed at because of you... Do let me know before August 1st, since I will be away for two months in Baroda.
Ravindra.'

You decide not to reply.

That night, Kausalya, Ulka, Urmi and Sushila, assistant to Mrs Sharma, come to your room after dinner with dog-eared notebooks and lemon tea.

You are their elder sister, the woman who knows hairy-chested men, crumbling-moon orgasms, stomach-tearing childbirth, deception, abandonment, loneliness, death.

They want you to prepare them for the twisted path that lies ahead, but you know you are too young, too vulnerable to give them the gift of that perspective.

Right now, all you have is the beginning of the understanding of a mystery.

When they finish reading their favourite poets, you merely recite what you have written over one hundred afternoons of aloneness at the library.

Somehow, not knowing the members of the caucus well enough makes it easier for you to open up.

'Nobody knows about this, my sisters, this is the world première of the thoughts of a little girl in a small village called Wada, a little girl overtaken by events. They are random two-line thoughts.'

Then you start reading from the diary you maintained in the library.

'How come there are two genders
but only one umbilical cord?'

'Why do brothers grow up and remember
that sisters are women?'

'If love binds, what sets you free?
When an orphan dies, who is happy?'

'If poetry does not lead you beyond words,
why read?
Why write?
If music does not lead you beyond sound,
why listen?
Why sing?
If living does not lead you beyond being human,
why live?
Why?'

The girls stare at you speechlessly.

There was nothing in your warm smile that hinted at so much self-scouring, and as an explanation, for the first time in your life, you discover the distance that allows you to talk in third person about your father, your brothers, your mother...you stop short of explaining the uncomfortable details of your married life. You hint at Ravindra's conquests around the world, the successful auto-didact from mill-town.

One Sunday morning that October, you are in the quadrangle of your hostel, sunning your long hair after your weekly head bath, mind drifting along black strands of thought. The children have finished their breakfast, since it is delivered to the hostel on Sundays.

Khot, the peon, has just finished telling you how he belongs to the village neighbouring Wada, and the legend of Maya, the woman who had the guts to confront the seniormost Brahmin in your village. It was a scene witnessed by eyes behind cacti, it is not myth. You tell him it is all hogwash, this so-called confrontation between castes. Maya was a lovelorn sister, that's all, and will he please shut up. Khot scampers away smiling, his beliefs about your strength confirmed rather than erased.

'*Kadaklakshmi*', he labels you in his mind.

Against the sun, the *darwaan* looks like a character from a mythological book, his turban a starched cloth temple top. He tells you about a visitor in the glasshouse, a rather clever device invented by Mrs Luthra. Here, everybody can see you and your visitor, but cannot hear you.

Your heart misses a beat when you see him.

The same cheekbones, the same beard, no smile.

You want to hug him, he is the only man you are allowed to touch at this age, but it cannot be. The grapnel claws of tradition sunk in your back have not been extracted yet.

You still haven't addressed him by his name. Ever.

Next to him is another familiar face. Gajanan. And next to Gajanan is a young girl. Blonde hair, deep lines from nostrils as delicate as petals to lips as precisely defined as bows, freckled fair skin, dress the colour of blood.

Ravindra introduces the two of you: 'Christine, this is Maya, my legal wife, Maya this is Christine, my agent in Paris. She wanted to meet you before we... I mean...she wants to marry me...'

The needle of the seismometer continues its boring up and down: you are relieved that no twinge of envy disturbs the steady rhythm of life inside you.

You smile at Christine and touch her hand, uncertain about any other form of greeting. She smiles back, her teeth a gleaming row. To Ravindra's surprise, you invite them all to your hostel, pointing out the landmarks on the way.

Ravindra has come under the guise of bringing the invitation cards to the exhibition of his new series, to be held to mark the seventh anniversary of his début.

'Very clearly, Mr Patil, exposed to a larger ecology of the mind and spirit during his sojourns abroad, is now ready to accept a more fundamental challenge. He pits his contemplative injunctions against the monological residue of the Cartesian tradition, inventing new stencils of form for the hermeneutics...'

Despite being highly strung, Ravindra cannot but get inebriated by the riot of colour on the campus. He saturates a canvas dryad with a sparking, fluttering *gulmohar* canopy for hair, a mermaid wearing powder blue jacaranda tattoos on her moist skin, a black mother of the universe with silver water tresses.

'What if you made this your home, famous-artist turned romantic-recluse, India's very own Gauguin...' you ask him, as you two stand on the edge of the valley.

In reply, he sniggers, 'Why go backward in life, Maya...from Paris to a hick town like Mahabaleshwar? Christine believes I can make Paris my home...'

When you reach the hostel, Sharan, a happy but quiet six-year-old, is playing with all his elder *didi*s and *dada*s, to whom he is the resident teddy bear. Sharan does not recognise Ravindra at all. This embarrasses Ravindra, since now the audience includes Kausalya and Mr Bhatkhande, who have dropped in with a special Sunday dessert for you.

At lunchtime, in the dining hall, you show off Ravindra's invite for the exhibition. Ravindra introduces Christine, the agent, and Gajanan, the friend who started it all. There are murmurs of appreciation, travelling abroad is still an exotic event for everyone, and Kunte, the art teacher, insists on showing Ravindra and gang his own charcoals.

While you walk back, wanting to be with Ravindra (you are sure this is the last time), he asks you a question you have never thought of, 'So...don't you miss what we did in the studio...or you have found somebody already...Christine has taught me so many new things about that...'

It takes you some time to understand he is talking about sex. About sheet lightning sparked off by turgid, wet nerves inside you. About vermillion orgasms under your eyelids. About the fruit of a million sighs celebrated by an ageing poet.

You imagine Christine and him in Paris. You imagine their athletic lovemaking like in the books of Parisians...you have forgotten already...must be Anaïs Nin and somebody called Miller. Then you revisit your appointments with an angry broom, your shame at being touted as a blind moth attracted to a hot poet, your anger with yourself for not being able to support your own child...and you realise the question has lost meaning, simply because you were so busy battling on other fronts.

Will those satin-sheet moments sprout again, demanding that you quench the thirst of two-inch-deep skin? Don't know. Everything in life has been unplanned; you will address the exigencies of the skin when they arise.

Later, as the five of you stand watching the sunset, Christine, alleged tutor of lovemaking, asks you, in halting English, if you still love Ravindra. Her voice has a question and a hint of supplication.

You wait before you answer. You want to tell the truth.

'There are many forms of love, Christine, but only one that can change human beings...that love I do not know yet...because in that love there is no I.'

She stares at you.

Did she not understand? Or did she think you were confused, or plain daft?

But her next question is one that will lodge inside you for years, a thorn suppurating in flesh.

'So in that way you do not love your son too, yes... or no?'

Inside you the silence is angry and confused one moment, full of acceptance the next. Just because the question came from a stranger did not make the question less potent.

Your love for Sharan is your love for yourself.

You walk up and down the corridors of your mind, trying to find a certainty, realise you do not have the answer.

She must be right: your love for Sharan is your love for yourself.

Gajanan grins. Ravindra laughs, puts his hand around Christine's waist.

The five of you walk towards the gates that can scratch noisy arcs on the dome of the copper sky.

Ravindra kneels down and kisses Sharan. You wish Ravindra all the best, you squeeze Christine's palm. You owe her a 'Thank You'. For doing something no one else had done. For waking you up to the tiny fault in your pursuit of light. Maybe some day you will meet her in the mother dream.

With a clang, the *darwaan* closes chapter number god-knows-which in your life.

❧ 24 ❧

Together Now: The Four Orders of Love

DURING THE NEXT CAUCUS MEETING, the sisters, Ulka and Urmi, who have studied a lot of *bhakti* literature, introduce you to the Four Orders of Love: servant for master; friend for friend; parent for child; spouse for spouse. They believe they have experienced only the second order, while you have experienced all.

It seems all your Orders of Love will be expressed through flat blue inland letters and rice paper envelopes. Sandhya has written about how lonely she is, how Sanjay has accepted his bank's offer for a transfer out of Bombay.

Did Sanjay love you like a servant loves his master? Was Sandhya the only Second Order Love in your life?

What about Sibling Love? Would the literature never acknowledge *Dada*?

Mahadevan and Sylvia mention in their letter that you are included in the little dream they are dreaming for themselves. They are planning to get married, but without ceremony, since the families are against an inter-religious marriage, and they are sure they have your *aashirwaad*.

The beautiful rice paper has Pankaj's ill-formed handwriting, apologising for not replying on time. He has had to visit his father, who was ill in Belgium. The terrible thing is, he might have to migrate too because his father is unable to cope.

You write back to everybody, describing how you have rediscovered your childhood paradise at the school. But you hatch a secret plan, and let Pankaj and *Maavshi* know that they should expect you in November.

Hari Niwas welcomes you with sunshine, sea breath and a juddering elevator.

Maavshi hugs you, Pankaj flings Sharan in the air but strains his back in the bargain, not realising that Sharan has put on weight in just six months. The faithfuls gather for another delectable party in the evening. You catch yourself being aware of being happy. You want to dance with all of them, and to your surprise, you feel so much at home now, you do!

Mr Ganguly, as he guides you around gently, whispers, 'I admire your courage, young lady, may god bless you.'

Varun mentions that his dad still asks after you, though he has a new Russian admirer, all blue eyes and blonde hair.

Then you pull out and hand over the little poems you have written for Sylvia and Mahadevan, having decorated the handmade paper from the New Era art class with fragrant dry leaves of eucalyptus and lemon. Sylvia kisses you on your cheek, sings your favourite song for you. Mrs Shah squeals in delight, asks you if you will indeed make a career out of writing. You laugh.

You don't need new careers, you are happy with your career in living.

The night grows inkier, fuzzier, faster, louder.

Pankaj, as is seemingly his habit, makes his announcement, and extinguishes the noise. 'Friends, this could well be our last party here for a long time to come. I have to go, as you all know, to Belgium, to look after my father. *Maavshi* insists on staying here and providing you an island for retreat...'

It is the right time for you to spring your surprise. 'Sorry to interrupt, Pankaj...but on behalf of all of you, I would like to publicly request *Maavshi* to accompany me to my new home...for the sake of Sharan's love, if not for mine.'

You can hear the odd car screaming down Marine Drive. Sharan's heart presses its metronome against your collarbone, just above the four-cupped metal stethoscope owned by Ravindra. Sylvia and Mahadevan stand hand-in-hand staring at *Maavshi*, as she stands at the kitchen door. Mrs Shah holds her gin glass at a precarious angle, and stares at *Maavshi*. Mr Ganguly pats down the nape hair, smiling at the drama unfolding before his bleary eyes, staring at *Maavshi*.

When she smiles, they burst into a huge congratulatory roar. When they leave there are threats of holding your January birthday party in Mahabaleshwar. The mind boggles at the thought, yet you cannot help smiling. Imagine the two 'U' sisters and Mrs Luthra watching you dance, worse still, stealing a swig of beer!

You have never sat in a car for six long hours, let alone in an old Chevrolet Impala.

The seats smell of artificial leather, the petrol fumes remind you of pica, your hunger for strange objects when you were pregnant with Sharan. Sharan sits in *Maavshi*'s lap, his huge eyes staring at this duplicated miracle. Yes, once upon a time, he had seen this scene from another moving thing, a train, where everything moves backwards when you stare at it.

Pankaj negotiates the *ghats* with practised ease. Cars are not allowed into the campus. So when the giant gates scratch against the ice-cold November sky, an eight-legged creature returns to Laburnum House instead of the usual six-legged one. Nobody is happier than Sharan at having his favourite grandmother back where he is. His mother is there with him, but sometimes she visits other universes, while his grandmother is always there, her eyes are only for him. He proudly introduces her to Manisha, his silent friend.

Mrs Luthra is quite impressed by Pankaj's Impala, his well-cut suit and the Antwerp address on his business card. This, after a visit by your husband who has a Parisian as his agent! In her mind, she hurriedly changes her assumptions about you. The original picture of you as a hapless discard morphs into a steel-spined youngster with the right connections.

You decide not to tell half-truths.

'Mrs Luthra, the closest but certainly not the legally correct description of Pankaj is as my younger brother, though we didn't meet each other till 1960.'

When the three of you sit overlooking the valley, it is Pankaj who speaks his mind. Despite the moment, his voice is steady. 'Maya*didi*, *Maavshi* is your responsibility now. *Maavshi*, Maya*didi* and Sharan are yours.'

The Impala vanishes behind the hump leading up to the school. *Maavshi* and you walk back, uncertain but happy.

'A giant cloud of leaden grey sorrow on the bent back

of a matchstick girl, her feet mired in a deep wet orange, a mixture of red soil, crushed *dhak* flowers and anger.'

That was how Ravindra painted you once. How much has changed!

If you were to imitate his style, you would paint a translucent woman in air, against a deep blue sky, with a hundred long arms, touching her son and the many members of her new family, relations without names, and instead of her heart, there would be a diamond bursting with light.

❧ 25 ❧
End of the Beginning

'CUT THE LOWER TENDON OF THE TONGUE and move the tongue constantly; rub it with butter, lengthen it with an iron instrument. By practising this, the tongue becomes long enough to reach the space between the eyebrows. Then practise turning it inwards and reaching the holes of the nostrils opening into the mouth. Close these holes with the tongue, stop inspiration, and gaze between the eyebrows. Now there is neither fainting, nor hunger, nor thirst, nor laziness, nor disease, nor decay, nor death.'

Did your father actually reach the top of the mountain he planned to reach?

Or did he use the power of his yogic postures to commit suicide, frustrated by his own lack of progress?

Just before he entered *nirvikalpasamaadhi* (did he, indeed?), did his brain flash a faded picture of a sloping-shoulders-black-pool-eyed girl called Maya?

Or did he mistake her for the sixth *chakra*, where resides Goddess Maya, the one that leads to all illusion?

You will not know. Your brother will not know.

Ravindra will not know. They are decent enough to send you the information that the body in Benaras had been positively identified as your father's body because he left a note for his eldest son. He was seventy years old when he died. If you want to shed tears, maybe this is the right time. With boring predictability, when the letter from your elder brother in Wada reaches you via Ravindra, it is July, and it is raining.

Silver threads bound earth and sky when he abandoned you, his favourite child. Even with his death, nothing has changed.

You, the *ersatz* orphan, are now a certified, blue-chip orphan. And you, the blue-chip mother are an anxious mother. You know in your bones, like your father did, that you have no control over what will happen in the future. You may not want to part from Sharan, but what if you have to? Silver threads bind father and mother. Christine, Ravindra's agent, who had come from across oceans, asked you just one question and exposed the chink in your pursuit of eternal bliss: your attachment to your son.

'Hold your canopy wide and firm, my *gulmohar*, I have no other protection against the coldness of this ancient rain.'

Pankaj has been diligently sending you beautiful cards on your birthdays. You write long letters in reply, expressing your sense of hollowness after your father's second death, the sense of severing one part of your consciousness, the sense of losing control all over again.

When you open his next letter, old rose petals, like paper dipped in dry blood, float out. Many lives ago, another young man had used paper to open his heart to you, under a lone, post-coital light bulb.

'Dear Mayadidi,

Here are some of the petals my sister Aditi sent me as her last message. She had had an arranged marriage, and we knew she was unhappy. I could see it in her eyes (they were like yours, with so many quiet stories hidden within), yet I was too young to fight against my own father, who probably was more worried about losing face in his community.

We still do not know where she went, we still do not know if she is alive. I am sorry you heard about your father's death this way... I only want you to always let me know if you are unhappy. Don't run away like my sister did, without giving me a chance to help you...swear by these petals.'

You cup the fragrance of Aditi's separation, and freedom, in your palms. But just round the corner is waiting the realisation, once again, that in the matters closest to your heart, practically nobody will be able to help.

Welcome to the Lone Battles Brigade.

❦ 26 ❦
The Last Betrayal, Almost

IT HAS BEEN TWO YEARS since Sharan has started practising with Mr Bhatkhande's students. Quiet Kausalya, whose ears, beautiful shell-like instruments of measurement, can differentiate between over a thousand JNDs ('Just Noticeable Differences', explains Mr Bhatkhande) between the highest and lowest audible tones, tells you with admiration that Sharan can hold a note at 550 Hz for longer than any other human being she has heard. He will be able to do this till his voice breaks at adolescence, she advises you.

Wise Mr Bhatkhande somehow sees the logical end of this kind of talent and feels sad for you. He has witnessed the pain that accompanies choice, in the case of his wife, and of his daughter. They chose different paths, they reached different disappointments.

That year, when school is about to be closed for summer, the State Minister for Culture, Gagan*rao* Bhide, whose daughter studies in the school, visits it as Chief Guest on Parents' Day. He listens to Sharan sing '*Kausalya suprajaa*' in praise of Lord Ram, in a voice like liquid gold, and his eyes grow moist.

'Will you sing at the annual convention of the Party?' he asks Sharan. Then glancing at you and doing a perfunctory *namaste*, he adds, 'Bring *Aai* along?'

You blurt out, 'No, please,' then pause. 'Actually I didn't mean it that way, but he is weak in his studies.'

Mrs Luthra gesticulates wildly while the State Minister, the delta of capillaries in his eyes growing redder, says, 'Okay, see for yourself...after all, we are servants of the people.'

Then you hear the same liquid gold voice saying, from behind your *pallu*,

'I want to go.'

Mrs Luthra glances at you archly, 'Sharan obviously understands what is good for him better than you know what is good for you, Maya!'

Under the State Minister's starched white *kurta*, his stomach shakes in silent laughter.

'How can this be? We were one, once upon a time, remember, your blood my blood, your lymph my lymph. (It all started with a woman rinsing her hair in a waterfall of light and a beer).'

Sharan returns late evening, feet black from playing in the mud. As he excitedly narrates his run down the left flank in the last football game of the season, you realise how you hate the depressing black soil, because you hate your son's desire to go away from you, and you hate your dependence on his desires.

The *shloka* mocks you.

'...*pita naiva me naiva maata cha janma...*'

'...neither father, mother nor birth...I am pure bliss...'

'Sharan, do you really want to sing before thousands of

people, my *beta*?'

He stops eating, pushes his lower lip out, his eyes grow moist. What to do? How to tell him, this is a game, you are a pawn, the winner is always somebody else, your mother has been through this?

In your mind flashes a thought that shocks you: you wanted to slap him so he would listen. It shocks you because you have never been hit or punished by your parents.

Didn't someone tell you long ago that all human beings are capable of the highest and the lowest that mankind itself is capable of? Maya, the goddess, who creates divisions, is divided. You don't wish to force your will on him, and yet you don't want him to go down a path that will change him as a human being.

When *Maavshi* finds you sitting at the feet of the *gulmohar* at night, she puts her arm around your shoulder. 'Missing Ravindra, *sona*?' You pat her hand, tell her what is really bothering you.

Maavshi shares your pain by sitting next to you.

The moon crumbles and makes the *gulmohar* sprout silver flowers instead of orange.

❧ 27 ❧
The Beginning of Another End

MRS LUTHRA IS ALL TOO HAPPY to grant you two days leave to accompany Sharan to the Annual Convention of Gagan*rao* Bhide's political party. You want *Maavshi* to accompany you, just for the fun of it. But she feels it would not be good for your reputation if your Laburnum House was left unshepherded. Like all events in your life, this event too will ascend the spiral of your life, and ask you uncomfortable questions.

The ride in the Ambassador car preceded by a police jeep is an unreal experience. Sharan enjoys it no end. The drive to Kolhapur, where the Party Convention is being held, ordinarily takes four hours. But a flat tyre and Sharan's delicate constitution necessitates frequent stops in the July heat. By the time you reach Kolhapur, you are more tired due to the excessive bowing and scraping your escorts indulge in than due to the physical strain of an eight-hour journey.

You reach the Public Works Department Guest House when it is dark, and Sharan is wilting. You hurriedly arrange for him to have a little dinner, and wash up yourself. As you sit down to unpack Sharan's clothes for the next morning, (you have bought him, your little prince, a dressy *sherwani*) you sense the presence of someone outside the door.

Suddenly, you rush down a mental corridor, helplessly folding up all the newspaper articles you have read about the new breed of politicians.

Absolute power corrupts absolutely.

Red-delta-eyed Gagan*rao* Bhide, liquor, late night, husbandless-white-thighed woman, *déjà vu*.

A decade ago, you had found yourself stranded in a poet's house, hobbled by your naïveté. You paid the price with sore ribs, a marriage that came apart at its seams, a layer of slime over your body. How can you be caught out again, even if you were temporarily blinded by your son's demands? You are thirty-five years old, for god's sake!

You decide you will use your old weapon, the language of the ex-masters, to castrate whoever stands before you.

'What is it?' You open the door and bark in English. Before you stands one more minion in white, another bowing and scraping specialist.

'*Saheb* wants to know if you can come...'

'Now? For what? Which *Saheb*? *Haan*?' He stands silent, head bowed.

You slam the door shut, unsure about how serious the situation will get.

Why the hell did you acquiesce to Sharan's stupid demand? For a moment you consider using a crying, weeping Sharan as your shield, then to your own surprise, cast that option away. You put off the lights, slide the latches on, and sit rigid at the edge of the bed, holding your *pallu* tight around your shoulder, your last lustproof vest.

Five minutes later, there is a knock on the door. You do not respond.

A few minutes later, the knock is repeated.

'What is the prob...' you shout, then stop mid-sentence.

Fortunately, and unfortunately, the voice behind the closed door is a familiar voice. And thankfully, behind that voice are many voices, two of them female.

You can pack up your secret weapon.

Krishna*rao* Khare, the exploiter who is fair to both genders, the state poet whose blow-ups adorned Ganapati festival *mandaps*, the man whose voice can stop a hummingbird in mid-flight.

His flesh hangs on his bones, but his appetite for encomiums is undiminished. 'I am very sorry to disturb you at this hour, Maya, when Gagan*rao* told me about your son, I thought you wouldn't mind if I congratulated you...'

There are polite introductions all round. Krishna*rao* explains to everybody how your spirited defence of his poetry changed the very complexion of the very first Sammelan after Maharashtra became an independent state.

You do not allow the half-truth to go unchallenged.

'Krishna*rao* exaggerates...it was his *haiku*s that created a furore.'

You grudgingly admire Gaganrao, who refuses to accompany Krishna*rao* at his whisky drinking. Maybe it is because Gagan*rao* is accompanied by his wife. You strike up a conversation with her, Shalini*tai*, and discover yourself liking her. She mentions that her husband has to work throughout the night for tomorrow's programme.

Gagan*rao* politely asks you if you do not want to

congratulate Krishna*rao* in return. After all, he is to be felicitated tomorrow on his 60th birthday, as well as for winning the USSR World Worker's Poet medal. You mumble something about living in the golden cage of a residential school, where the outside world is almost irrelevant.

'That's Maya for you, Gagan*rao*, always irreverent! She came from a small village, Gagan*rao*, and came to meet me, her father's favourite poet, and became as famous as the poet...do you still write for the magazine where you first skinned me alive, *haan*, Maya?'

His laughter is still like rolling thunder, his voice is still the distillate of summer, his tonsils are still sacs filled with venom.

You realise how difficult it is to cast aside the psychological domination built since childhood, the seduction of that voice, the thousand-foot stature constructed jointly by your father and you.

You smile, but refuse to get drawn into his trap.

You wear your sari on top of your head throughout, and then ask Gagan*rao*'s permission to be with Sharan. The little boy needed his rest, even if the older men did not. Krishna*rao* laughs again, raising his glass of whisky in tribute to your spirit. You whisper to the minion's wife that you need her to sleep with Sharan and you, because you can rarely sleep peacefully in alien surroundings. Some discussions later, she joins you, insisting that she sleep on the floor.

You make sure your door is latched firmly from within.

You do not want Krishna*rao*'s birthday to be celebrated as it was a decade ago.

The actual ceremony is an experience that you will not

easily forget. Neither Sharan nor you have ever witnessed crowds like these. They are constantly milling around, spread across a flat land divided by a million colourful bamboo poles. The further you look the more like a painting they appear. If Ravindra were here, he would have seen a two-inch-deep ferruginous burnt sienna, slashed by vertical off-white stubs of broken sound. The crowd creates a white noise, a huge hum that is interrupted by the Party volunteers shouting instructions.

Someone sprints across with an aluminium jug of water for a pregnant woman who has fainted. The marigolds on the *mandap* wilt under the sun's ire. At the end of two interminable hours, the Chief Minister arrives, his Ambassador car whipping up a minor storm of dust. The crowd senses that someone important has arrived, the applause explodes in dull clumps. The meeting begins with Sharan's singing, but the sound system has been created for long, loud rhetoric, and his *shloka* is lost on the restive crowds. There is no applause, except an encouraging pat on his head by the Chief Minister and a quick photo-session, where Gaganrao insists on including you.

You decide to leave the moment Sharan's singing is over, despite Gaganrao's requests. The more the distance between your family and Krishnarao, the safer you are.

When you reach New Era School, Sharan sulks, refusing to eat, disappointed by the effect of his first public appearance outside of the school.

'Stop this,' you scream in your mind, 'Stop. This is not how and why I dreamt dreams for you.'

Unfortunately, everybody's dreams are different. They don't obey imagined guidelines.

His pride is restored the next day when the photograph

appears in the *Mahabaleshwar Times*. He flanks Gagan*rao* Bhide, Krishna*rao* Khare, and his mother, his photo is there because he is one of the 'youngest accomplished classical singers training under Shri Bhatkhande at the New Era School...'

He is not privy to your conversation with *Maavshi*, when you explain your angry, hair-raising tale. Ulka and Urmi want to know if the famous poet Krishna*rao* Khare said anything of import.

You smile a quiet 'No'.

In Bombay, three years after Ravindra last saw you, *Nana* has died in his drunkenness, smashed by a car going the wrong way on a one-way street near his mill, still smiling about a joke he has cracked. Ravindra considers calling you, then chances upon your photograph with Krishna*rao* and Gagan*rao*, and decides it confirms your alleged infidelity. In his mind, this far outweighs all that you did for him, and he finalises his migration to Paris and his marriage to Christine.

During the next year there is an increasing number of demands for Sharan's performances. Audiences love the novelty of a young boy remembering the intricacies of commonly known songs. You are getting tired of accompanying him out of the campus, to Satara, to Panchgani, to Poona. You hate the hypocrisy, the fake politeness, the palpable lust for an unaccompanied woman, the casualness of the demands. You hate the feeling of exploiting *Maavshi*'s presence as a substitute for yours at Laburnum House.

The next Saturday, at your weekly private dinner at the House, you are at breaking point. This is not possible. Just when you thought everything was under control. Just when you had managed to live on your own meagre ability instead of a diamond merchant's or a Paris-returned artist's. Just when you were happy that your choice of profession favoured your son more than you.

Your own son, how can your son not listen to you?

Mr Bhatkhande's voice is quiet. 'Maya, my child, don't fret. Your son was born a "creature of stillness". He was born quiet, in order to better listen to the music of the universe. And if he is destined to join in the harmony, why worry? After all, he is just chasing his own muse.'

'So what do I do, *kaka*, let him be a puppet in the hands of these parasites of culture? I don't mind him pursuing music, but I believe I know what would happen if he pursued fame instead. I know because I have seen his father...and a so-called poet do the same...' You break into sobs of exasperation. *Maavshi* places an affectionate hand on your back.

You walk out into the cold of the night, exposing your heart to the bony grip of the winter air. The cicadas lengthen the uncomfortable gaps in your logic. The security guard's whistle recedes, its resonance congealing in black circles.

Black. The colour of your thoughts right now. A black that's worse than the one that enveloped you the night you got pushed out of the Patil household.

Thankfully, Mr Bhatkhande is too old to be scared of a young woman's tantrums. He follows you, he has an answer that you hate. 'Let him pursue his muse till he either tires of it or finds his path through it.'

'Did you let Kausalya follow her path?' you ask, the unnecessary anger in your voice surprising you.

He smiles, 'Yes, Maya, whether you believe it or not,

yes. It was she who decided she did not want to take on the world, unlike her mother.'

You are so disturbed you miss this sudden reference to his wife. It will be explained to you under this very tree many years later.

'Maya, my *gurubandhu*, Pandit Arolikar, you understand, we trained under the same guru, continues to teach a select batch of students. He is in Indore. Rather than let Sharan drift along these nonsensical populist performances, let him undergo genuine *taalim*, let him understand that music is a ruthless mistress. This will solve your worries of him being exploited by unrelated human beings. It will allow him to decide if his instinctive hunger for music is a passing phase...or his *dharma*.'

❧ 28 ❧
Your Father's Daughter

ACCORDING TO LEGEND, Diwali is celebrated to mark the homecoming of Rama, Lakshman and Sita from fourteen years of exile.

This Diwali is the beginning of your son's exile, even though you may not know it yet.

During the holidays, the Bhatkhandes and you leave for Indore via Bombay. The only real homecoming refers to Pankaj, who is returning from Antwerp after five long years. *Maavshi* and you have requested him to come earlier, so you can all meet in Bombay. You have also written to Sandhya and Sanjay, asking them to call you at Pankaj's number, the six-digit code to your independence.

You leave Sharan in *Maavshi*'s care at Hari Niwas, and go to the airport to receive Pankaj. It is the same airport where you last said goodbye to a man who was uncertain about the power of his sperm. Pankaj appears tired, and when you hug him, you can feel his ribs.

When he reaches Hari Niwas, it is his turn to be surprised. All his friends are waiting. A joyous cry shakes

Floor Five. Though the party never reaches its earlier bonhomous versions, it does transform into a confluence of two opposing streams of music. Sylvia sings jazz, and under her father's gentle goading, shy Kausalya replies with a *thumri*.

Smoke-plus-sunshine-on-hay-plus-nostalgia voice meets stream-of-light-bounding-down-the-Sahyadris voice.

Sharan is grown up enough to stay awake late at night, and as you watch him gawping in fascination, you reassure yourself you are forcing him to travel towards the right destination.

Mrs Shah listens in fascination to Mr Bhatkhande's explanations about the physical difference between *Aum* and *Amen*, about male and female sounds, about male and female sense organs. The ear is female, it receives without distortion even before you are born, that's why it never suffers from acoustical illusion. The eye is male, it darts out, licks surfaces, is easily fooled. Entire cultures can be male or female, aggressive or peaceful, based on their use of eyes and ears.

You hug Sandhya and Sanjay. Sandhya, believe it or not, is the supervisor in her tiny factory, and Sanjay is doing well in his bank: they had even sent him to Hong Kong for further exposure.

Varun is even quieter than before, and you can see him smiling and whispering to Pankaj many times during the night. Mr Ganguly is fascinated by Kausalya's singing, and wants to know if it is too late for him to start learning. She breaks into laughter as musical as her voice.

Pankaj insists on letting his guests from out of town experience the true taste of Bombay. The November weather is crisp. The city looks gorgeous from the little restaurant at Malabar Hill, from the gardens of Aarey Milk Colony, from the quiet guest-houses in Madh Island. In your sixteen years in Bombay, you yourself have not absorbed the city as you do now.

Pankaj also accompanies the five of you to Indore.

He changes the train tickets to First Class. In your memory, that journey of fifteen hours becomes a journey in Fairy Tale class. *Maavshi* has put together the most potent winter snacks. Pankaj has brought along toys that make Sharan swoon. Mr Bhatkhande has fascinating tale after fascinating tale to share with you all.

He shuts the door of the cabin and puts off the lights, so that you may hear his gimmick ('Oh, it is no more than a gimmick, don't you worry') better. He starts chanting '*Aum*', the sound emerges from his stomach, but then, magically above the steady drone, you start hearing wisps of flute.

When Kausalya puts on the light, the rest of you are dazzled.

Inside you, it stirs memories of what your father could do with a blackened mirror. Wada's only catoptromancy practitioner.

So many worlds, so many mysteries.

After much cajoling from *Maavshi*, Pankaj decides to fascinate Sharan, and the rest of you, with his magic tricks. Pankaj pulls one coin each out of Sharan's ears, his empty shirt pockets. Sharan squeals in delight, begs for more. At Surat station, Pankaj scares you by waving at you with Sharan in his arms from the platform, even as the train pulls out, and when you scream in panic (as you did for your husband a long while ago on receding memory tracks), he runs and catches the train.

Sharan cannot control his glee. His own mother is fooled! This is unbelievable fun!

If any of you knew what a Kirlian photograph was, and if it were possible to expose a Kirlian photograph of that little compartment of that train in November 1972, the result would have been a gigantic incandescent flare. Where *Maavshi*'s hand touches Sharan's head, where your hand touches Kausalya's hand, where Pankaj's hand touches Mr Bhatkhande's shoulder, where all the small flares of affection become one huge flare of love.

Between Khajuri Bazaar and the Bada Ganapati Mandir in Indore, is a quiet leafy lane, a cul-de-sac.

This is Mr Bhatkhande's domain. As you all move towards the end of the lane, he leads, mumbling that he hopes the address is right, touching an old *peepal* tree with thousands of white threads of reverence around its trunk. But he need not have worried. Even before you reach the *haveli* and see the board 'Pandit Arolikar School of Music', you can hear the school. Five or six voices, young and old, are practising. Rivers of sound, thin and thick, smooth and gnarled, criss-cross, mingle, disappear into new sounds.

The climb up the narrow staircase tires out Mr Bhatkhande. When you finally reach the top, a servant beckons all of you to a room away from where the students are sharpening their voices. Sharan stares at them, but they are oblivious to extraneous stimuli. The winter sun floods the room with watery light; the chairs are uncomfortable, the ceiling low, therefore, when Pandit Arolikar enters, to all of you, he appears to be a giant who has stepped out of mythology.

He is a big man, his *dhoti* and *kurta* crisp and white.

He stands against the sun, enveloped by cool white flames. His face has a glow partially hidden by his flared moustache. His eyes are remote; when he is looking at things, he is also looking at something within himself.

Later, Mr Bhatkhande will explain that the speciality of the Indore *gharana* is its insistence that every artist judge music in his inner mirror, that his soul sing for itself.

Look within before you look without.

All of you scramble and stand, hands folded in a polite '*Namaste*'.

Only Mr Bhatkhande takes his own time to come to his feet. Panditji hugs him, holds him at arms length, and mutters, '*Mhaataara, re mhaataara*...you old bandicoot... how many years now...fifteen, twenty...?!' They hug each other again, and in the faint light, you can sense their tears of joy.

The servant offers you all gigantic steel glasses of steaming hot, saffron-laden milk. The steam serpents stand like question marks, their spines supported by the cold air.

Mr Bhatkhande and Pandit*ji* sit on opposing chairs and speak in whispers. It appears that Mr Bhatkhande is the one who is making Pandit*ji* laugh, and what a laugh! You remember a phrase translated from Sanskrit literature: they called such laughter 'condensed thunder'. It was meant to be the laughter of Lord Shiva, the originator of all music.

The rest of you watch this meeting of friends as if it's a play being enacted specially for you.

Finally, Mr Bhatkhande pulls little Sharan towards himself, then holds him like an exhibit in front of Pandit*ji*.

'Trimbak, Sharan is like my grandson. You have to

train him, no...sorry, you must train him, for my sake, for maybe our guru*ji*'s sake. He can hold a note longer than my own daughter can, but I do not know if he will be able to hold it against the forces that sell music in the marketplace... I lost the right to say anything the day I gave up my pursuit...'

His regret hangs in the air. What had the two shared? What had they parted over? Had they fought when Mr Bhatkhande chose to become the teacher of classical music in a school? Had Pandit*ji* abused him for dishonouring the memory of their guru? Had they fallen in love with the same woman?

Who was to know?

Pandit*ji* leans forward. His face is now inches away from Sharan's.

Pandit*ji*'s stare drills two holes into Sharan. 'Little one, do you love music?'

Sharan stares back at Pandit*ji*.

'Yes.'

'Do you love music more than anything else?'

'Yes.'

One pair of black pools hides naiads and dry trilobites of memories, the other hides the harmony of the universe, as well as experience acknowledged and honoured by a *Padmashri* award.

'Okay, do you love music more than...A*ai*?'

Sharan's pools overflow, his lower lip quivers. He turns, glances at you, then stares back at Pandit*ji*.

He stands silent, his spine straight, his hands locked behind his back, left foot rubbing right calf, wrestling someone inside himself. The smiles on the faces of the others wilt. They had believed it was light-hearted banter, this is turning out to be a battle of wills. You can feel the heat of *Maavshi*'s stare, Pankaj's stare, Kausalya's stare, on the back of your neck...

Remember that Sharan forced you to eat iron-rich mud during your pregnancy to forge pistons inside his heart.

Remember he did not respond to his father's puerile attempt to be AWOL during his birth.

Remember that he is *both* the sons of Mother India you saw in a darkened theatre twelve years ago: the quiet submissive and the headstrong impulsive.

'What must I do...to prove my love?' he asks Pandit*ji* in return.

Pandit*ji* smiles, shrugs, runs a serrated knife on your heart.

'Not meet *Aai* for many years, maybe.'

'Why?' replies Sharan.

This time, Pandit*ji* laughs till there are tears in his eyes. He looks skywards, and then at Mr Bhatkhande, '*Devaa re devaa*...why must I meet myself in my old age...be asked the very questions I asked my guru...you remember?'

Mr Bhatkhande nods, touches the lobe of his ear in a gesture of respect for their teacher.

Then Pandit*ji* turns to Sharan, holds his palms in his huge hands, and says, 'Because you can have only one mother...every human being can have only one mother at a time, you understand that, don't you? If you accept music, she will be your mother from now on...though she will behave exactly the opposite of Maya here. She won't feed you, you will feed her. You will feed her your discipline, your fears, your arrogance, and then, years later, if and when all your pride has disappeared, she will bless you.'

Instead of being cowed down by Pandit*ji*'s answers, he asks one more question.

Only a child can do this. 'Only my Sharan can do this.'

'For how long do I have to stay with you...?'

'Not with me...' Pandit*ji* interrupts him, bulldozing him towards a decision.

Sharan somehow understands his error.

'How long do I have to stay...with music?'

'Ten years, fifteen...who knows how long it will take for you to understand what real music is...'

Then Pandit*ji* turns to you and speaks, 'This is not a game I play, Maya, this is penance... I don't teach music that sells... I teach music that points at something beyond our puny lives...you can take it or leave it...but do make a decision...so I don't waste my time.'

An old anger rises inside you. 'How dare you be so cruel to a young child...and what do you, sir, know of penance...I know someone who spent nights in a cremation ground...unmoved by the contemptuous shrieks of an entire village...' Your response is throttled by your sense of respect for Mr Bhatkhande, Pandit*ji*, the unknown wishes of your son...you are as confused as Ravindra was when he returned to fetch you from Pankaj's house.

Your son, of course, is neither confused nor angry. He is more resolute than you will ever be. He wants to win this battle of wills at any cost. Inside him is a grandfather who feared nothing.

He stares at Pandit*ji* without blinking, turns to you, his eyes moist, till you look away. Then you hear his accursed liquid gold voice.

'*Theek hai.*' 'It's okay'.

'So can *Aai* leave now?', Pandit*ji* tightens the screws.

You get up and hug Kausalya, you can't bear this.

The formalities are completed while you hide your face in Kausalya's shoulder, smelling the starch in her new blouse. You feel *Maavshi*'s warm palm on your back. Pankaj brings in a bag with Sharan's clothes. Mr Bhatkhande helps Sharan tie the '*ganda*', the thread of discipleship, on his wrist. A four-cupped stethoscope that hangs around your neck transferred you from your mother to Ravindra. An umbilical cord tied you to Sharan instead of to Ravindra. But now...just a piece of thread... red thread...that's all...that's all it takes to transfer the relationship of your son from you to mother music.

When you turn around, finally, Sharan is staring at you. You kneel before him. (Remember, many years ago, your father kneeled in the slush as he departed?)

You hug him till you can feel his heart against your ribs.

You hold Sharan at arm's length, like your father did. (Remember your father unhooked your arms when you clutched him?)

'Promise me you will not give up your dream?' (Remember you too made a promise you still haven't understood completely?)

Father and daughter and daughter and son locked in a slow spiral of separations. Father had to deny himself the love of his daughter so he could pursue his goddess, daughter has to deny herself the love of her son, so he can pursue his goddess.

Sharan is more grown up than you were.

'I don't know *Aai*, I'll try...but whatever happens, I will come back to you. Wait for me.'

There is just one good omen: no rain.

❧ 29 ❧
Mother Nature

YOU MANAGE TO HOLD BACK THE TEARS only till you are out of the lane.

The parting lasted not more than an hour. For fifteen hours before that, you were being fattened for the kill on a diet of camaraderie, love and affection.

Plus the garnishing of memories over eleven years: Sharan's puckered face after he first suckled you and fell into a deep sleep; him standing akimbo next to you as you sat and forced *chaklis* out of a constipated squeezing machine; chasing the bitter fruit on Diwali day in a tiny *dhoti*; singing before a crowd of thousands, unafraid of their inattention.

Drained by the storm within you, you sit on the platform at the feet of the ficus. The rest stand around, unable to help you. Their affection cannot bridge this pain of separation.

Your mind makes futile attempts to apportion blame where it does not belong.

You have a suspicion that Mr Bhatkhande engineered this deliberate separation between mother and son.

Maybe Pankaj too was jealous of your attachment to Sharan. Or perhaps Kausalya had nothing but envy at being upstaged as the best singer in the school. Deep inside, you know it is all nonsense, but the thoughts provide a distracting balm to the dull ache.

Mr Bhatkhande insists on showing Pankaj the charms of the town, reciprocating Pankaj's gesture in Bombay. You join in gamely, despite the pain. Is this what your father felt? Did he drag a heart with a spike of guilt and anger shoved in it, as he wandered on his pilgrimage? Did he, after Ramtek, come here, where Mr Bhatkhande has dragged you, to this heartbreakingly beautiful island of Omkareshwar that looms out of nowhere in the midst of the great river Narmada?

Did he pray for his child, as you pray now, for the first time in your life, before one of the twelve most sacred *jyotirlings*?

'Oh Lord Shiva, I have abandoned the fruit of my womb, he is in pursuit of music, music that you created at the beginning of the universe, so look after him, look after him, look after him.'

You leave a trail of quiet lament at the Kanch Mandir, at the Lal Bagh Palace, at the Museum. Mr Bhatkhande is visiting the Indore that survives in his nostalgia. He talks about singing for a play in 1922, where the entire set of clothes and props was provided by the King of Indore himself, about his Indore Public School's magnificent 100-odd-acre campus, about the quality of the cotton grown in the fields adjoining Indore.

Nobody says anything to you about Sharan.

That night, after many years, you retreat into the dream of mothers. Sons and daughters will have to leave, explains a Mexican mother with a red and black *serape* and many hundred wrinkles, to discover the sky that has their own stars and their own constellations, and then they will come back, not to worry.

She does not say how long you will have to wait.

You spot *Mai* and your mother too, tending to different young mothers, smiling at you knowingly, confident that you will overcome.

You return to Pandit*ji*'s school before leaving Indore. The others accompany you, unsure of what you want, huddled together, worried that a closed chapter will be opened.

You bend down to touch Pandit*ji*'s feet, your ears straining to catch Sharan's voice among a dozen voices, and ask, 'Pandit*ji*, will he find his way in life through music?'

Pandit*ji*'s reply is cruel but correct, 'Who are you and I to ask, and what will you and I do even if we know the answer?'

A French woman with blonde hair asked you another question about your son, remember, and it meant the same thing.

❧ 30 ❧
Missives, Responses

YOU CONSTRUCT Sharan's days at the music school like a jigsaw puzzle, by assembling fragments of information given by Mr Bhatkhande, who, for twenty long years trained under the same guru along with Pandit*ji*. Mr Bhatkhande believes Pandit*ji* would be following the same routine even now. Other pieces of the jigsaw are provided by Sharan's letters, painstakingly written, in the light of a flickering lantern (your imagination again!).

Sharan gets up at five in the morning, he has to, as the youngest disciple. He has to draw water from the well, fill the woodfire boiler, light the fire and then get ready before it's time for *riyaaz*.

He now wears a *langot*, traditional Indian underwear, because he has to perform traditional Indian exercises. Pandit*ji* is a great believer in physical fitness as a necessary condition for the practice of music. So Sharan does *dands*, the arched push-ups, and *baithakhs*, the sit-ups that are the Indian wrestler's staple.

He is unused to the large quantity of milk that is

considered a standard part of the diet, and for days on end, suffers from diarrhoea. His practice cannot get affected: for Pandit*ji*, the body itself is an instrument of music, and if it's not in harmony, well, we must get it back into harmony. Even in his weakened state, Sharan has to keep up his practice. His voice is a squeak, but he is not excused. Powerful ayurvedic herbs help Sharan recover. But his colleagues tease him, when they sleep in their dormitories.

As far as Pandit*ji* is concerned, anything that batters the ego and subsumes it to the goddess of music is welcome.

'Dearest Aai,

Do not worry about me. I am fine. The classes are not different from Bhatkhande uncle's classes in school. I like singing. But the practice lasts very long. The food is not tasty like Maavshi ajji's or yours. My friends are good. I think of you all the time. When I fell ill, they teased me, because I used your old sari to cover myself at night. I let them laugh.

('And I? I live only because I hope some day I will see you again, you are the only part of me that is untouched by the dirt in my past.')

Your son,
Sharan
November '72'

The practice is relentless. It lasts for ten hours every day. The slightest lack of attention is punished. Pandit*ji* is someone who is described as a 'shataavadhaani'...one who is capable of being simultaneously aware of a hundred events. He has a unique method: he sits on the ground, legs folded in a classical *sahajasan*, in the centre of a circle created by his sitting students. He can detect the slightest change in pitch in the voices between his twelve elite wards. The moment that happens he uses the whips of a thin cane to remind the offending boy. The legs of the boys are covered with welts, darkening marks of dishonour.

His idea of teaching music is making it part of your son's metabolism...a healthy human heart makes no errors in its rhythm over a lifetime, neither should your son's voice.

'*Dearest* Aai,
  I have learnt four raags completely. Today Guruji paid me a compliment. Guruji says this is good progress for two years spent here. I dream of you. When it is cold, I still wrap your sari around me. I will become a good singer, I think.

  ('I have wrapped the memory of every moment of your life around me, nobody can penetrate my armour, nobody can touch me, neither *Maavshi* nor Pankaj nor Kausalya nor Bhivaji.')

  I love you Aai, *wait for me.*
  Sharan
  March '74'

'*Dearest* Aai,
  I am depressed because for no fault of mine I have to start my riyaaz differently. Guruji says my voice has changed because I am becoming an adult, and I must start the saadhana all over again.

  ('Yes, many years ago, Kausalya has warned me about this eventuality.')

191

Whatever happens now, I will now not give up music.

I love you Aai. I now understand what sacrifices you made to protect and keep me happy. Yesterday, I had a strange dream. I saw somebody beating you while I was in your arms, but I never felt anything. Then the man went away in the sky.

I love you Aai, wait for me.

Sharan.

March '75'

Every passing year, he unearths memories and draws his own conclusions. You worry that he is becoming an adult too soon.

('Listen, just because I lost my father when I was twelve and my mother when I was, what, twenty? doesn't mean you have to behave as if you have neither. I want you to follow your dream, because I did not even know what it means to own a dream of my own... I just lived out a script written for me by someone else').

'Dearest *Aai,*

I don't know how to start; I don't know how to end. I want to live with my music, see what it does to me. I'm sure you don't mind. I am a terrible son, but music is also a terrible mistress. But Aai, I promise you, I am not running away like Baba *did.*

Chaitanya, one of the boys, started teasing me that Baba *had not come with me when I joined the school or that he doesn't write letters like you do. So I beat him up (I have become very strong with all the exercises I do every morning!). When Guruji called us together for an enquiry, I told him I don't mind being whipped a hundred times for singing a wrong note, but I will not listen to this kind of dirt. I am not going to take punishment like you did...why should I? It is not my error, is it, that Baba ran away?*

('I want to know why men run away at all. They are hunters aren't they, with more muscle, emergency pouches of testosterone, sinewy deltoids, powerful thighs? Why do they always run away first and then supply the explanations?')

I will keep coming back to you, because I learnt my music from you.

Look after yourself, Aai, I know you will not misunderstand me. With your blessings, I shall be a good musician soon. Isn't that what you wish too? The day Guruji allows me to see you, I will rush to you.

Pranaam *and love,*
Sharan.
February '76'

The iron in the iron-rich mud you swallowed during your pregnancy has been annealed in the crucible of his memories. It has entered his nerves, like the cotton entered and softened your father-in-law's mind and the turpentine entered your husband's heart.

Sharan means surrender, but that meaning will play its hand only at the end of your story, not his. Sharan will not surrender to circumstances, he will bend it around his unyielding will.

'Dearest *Aai,*
Have to tell you about my first public concert in Pune. I asked Guruji if I could speak about you before I

started my performance...because there would never be a second first performance.

So I explained to the audience how you taught me to listen to the universe even while I was in your womb...the audience liked my singing. Even Chaitanya, who has been jealous of me, admitted that it was a good performance. He says, "You sing with your heart, not with your voice."

I couldn't explain it, but I felt your presence during that entire night. It was like being immersed in childhood again, you holding me and me listening to your heartbeat and listening to you humming...rhythm and the melody together again, taal *and* laya, *as Guru*ji *says, the male and female aspects of music.*

Pranaam Aai,

Sharan.

April '76'

That is one letter you know everything about. Unknown to him, you will be very close to him that night.

'Dearest and most beautiful Aai,

*For the first time in my life, I was made to accompany Guru*ji *on stage as his new* shaagird. *He had been invited to perform at the Benaras Music Festival at the Sankat Mochan temple. They say it has the maximum number of connoisseurs of music, yet it is free for all. They have taken to task even all-time greats. You are aware that Benaras represents one of the oldest* gharanas *of music, aren't you?*

So I was tense.

But one amazing thing happened the morning before.

At dawn, I had gone to see the river Ganga with my other gurubandhu, *Chaitanya. We have become good friends now.*

We went out into the river on a boat. It was like a lake, a kilometre wide, so utterly quiet. They say it is called Kashi, because it is the City of Light.

('I don't know if you know, my little one, but your grandfather gave up his life there, in pursuit of life.')

And along with dead bodies and vultures and dirt, I saw bamboos floating in the river. And I asked the boatman if they were the bamboos that came with the biers of the dead bodies. And he said, no, they keep bamboos floating in the middle of the river so if birds get tired crossing the river they can rest.

And I thought, that's like Aai. *If she were in Benaras she would have thought of something like this.*

All your life, you allowed everybody a resting place till they discovered where they have to fly off to.

Isn't that true? You allowed Baba *a resting place till he discovered the strength to go off and become an international artist.*

And you humoured me and spoilt me and strengthened me and allowed me to fly off so I could find my own calling, my own vocation.

So I sat there in the boat and I stared at the rising sun as the flanks of city were bathed in gold.

The City of Light.

And as I sat there, with the sound of conches attempting to wake up the gods, with the boatman's oar churning liquid metal, and the breeze snuffling against my skin, for a moment, or perhaps for many moments, my sense of myself vanished. There was nothing except light. I don't know how to describe the feeling.

('You don't have to my baby, you don't have to, I have known it since I was nine years old!')

There was no fear of the concert, no ill-will against Chaitanya, no memory even of you...it was magical.

It was as if, for a few moments, I had become light.

When we returned, I said to myself, "If I am light, then why I am I worried about success and failure? If music is a mother, as Guruji keeps saying, why would she measure me and judge me...you never did. You never demanded that I succeed, why would music?"

If music is my mother, she would merely accept. She would provide me a floating bamboo in the middle of the vast lake of life, till my exhausted limbs rediscovered their strength.

That's why that night when I sang at Sankat Mochan, the temple of Lord Hanuman, who surrendered his ego to Lord Ram, I said to myself, "I surrender to you, mother, whatever your name is, Maya, or Music or Ganga, you are all the same, I surrender to you, you have flowed across time, and you have seen all human beings and their puny talent, and you know some who scaled the ladder of that talent to understand what you understand, and some who scaled the ladder of their talent to thump their chests...not realising that they had climbed just one stretch of a mountain...so flow through me...let me be your conduit of light...please, please."

After that, I was not tense. Music flowed through me, the Ganga flowed through me, you flowed through me. I was not there most of the night. Sounds stupid, na, Aai, when I write it? Also, sounds fake? I know you will never laugh, but perhaps you don't believe me either?

But for that night, it was true, really really true, Aai. After that, even when they applauded and even Guruji asked me to sing solo, which is considered a big step for a student, I did not feel tense or worried or even proud.

There is very little to feel proud about...but there is so much to feel happy about.

The only other thing I remember was an old lady in white. She came to me after my performance, and said, "That was brilliant beta, *but remember even emotion is a limitation in music."*

I didn't understand what she meant, maybe it is like the shloka *you taught me, it reveals its meaning as you open yourself to newer experiences.*

It's not a riddle we cannot solve, it's a truth we cannot see...

A hundred pranaams, *my first teacher.*

We will meet soon.

Your first shishya,

Sharan.

June '78'

'Dearest and most beautiful Aai,

Last night, Guruji was ill. This is the first time I have seen him ill. He has always been so strong. When everybody left, I told him, "Guruji, I have to do something for you. You have been my father for seven years now. I have no knowledge to heal your illness, but I have the knowledge that you gave me. Tell me, what should I sing for you...what can I make my voice and my heart do for you so you feel better...?"

And he said, "Remember I taught you a very old and difficult bandish *in* raag Maaru Bihaag? *It is known to cure depression. If you sing it well, maybe this rust that has encrusted my soul will dissolve...I too am tired..."*

So I kissed his fingers and I touched my earlobe as a mark of respect ('I know, I have seen you do it another time, another place, but you don't know!') and I said to myself "Is it possible?"

Then I said to myself, "No, I have to make it possible."

When I finished, I didn't know where I was. I had stopped singing, and next to me was Guruji, laughing like thunder, laughing with his face to the sky.

He shouted, "Kaivalya, I fulfilled my promise to you Kaivalya!"

Who is Kaivalya, Aai...do you know?

Anyway it felt good, to be able to do something for someone I respect so much.

See you soon,

Sharan.

December '78'

('Kaivalya is Mr Bhatkhande, my child, your other music teacher, he was the one who helped me help you discover your destiny...despite my stupid remarks.')

You tie the letters with a satin ribbon and wrap them in your childhood secret: the green petticoat shot with capillaries of pain. A wrapping paper that lasts for a lifetime.

❧ 31 ❧
The Spiral Curves Upon Itself

AS THE SCHOOL LURCHES from season to season, admission fervour to admission fervour, you draw more and more into yourself even while you accept greater responsibility. You start looking after the library, it rekindles your passion for books, takes your mind off Sharan's absence.

It's a simple enough job, and it adds a bit to your salary. All you do is keep a record of the books borrowed. Soon, you discover things beyond books. The library brings you in touch with the unsavoury aspects of the school. The senior students include sons of influential politicians and bureaucrats, who have grown cynical about the post-Independence slogans of 'eradicating poverty', 'serving the nation' and 'preserving the heritage'. The youngsters carry the poison of power in their blood, sense that Mrs Luthra has a soft belly, dare to look upon you as an easy target.

Unfortunately for them, in Girangaon, you have heard enough scatology and references to pudenda to last a lifetime. Thankfully for you, you know that every human being carries in the heart the highest and the lowest that the race believes in. You have experienced both the smallness and largesse of Krishna*rao*, the generosity of *Nana* the grandfather and the anger of *Nana* the father-in-law...even your own selfish desire to hold on to your son.

You stick to your old technique of sharing what you like, perfected in another library many years ago. 'Come, sit in the sun, let's enjoy the warmth of an idea that allows you to look at the world afresh, the softly beating heart of an elegant phrase, the steely thrust of an insight.'

Slowly, the less cynical ones reach out, start reading the books you have recommended, discuss them with you. As their numbers increase, the mischief grows less. The older teachers are curious about your confidence. They grudgingly accept your tact. You appear to have a very different starting point when dealing with all human beings.

Some even mention it to Mrs Luthra that you be nominated to the School Welfare Committee that looks after student-teacher relationships.

Mrs Luthra is only too glad to agree: she has been fascinated by your uncommon past. There is a certainty in you that she seeks in herself.

In the second year after Sharan's departure, Mrs Luthra requests that you sacrifice your November holidays and accompany the school trip to Ganapatipule, the famous beach resort in Konkan. Your knowledge of the region and the language will be an asset.

You accede to her request. You are aware that Pankaj is not expected that year, so returning to the flat in Bombay isn't very attractive. Neither is the idea of staying on the campus, haunted by the memories of Sharan: this is where he stumbled, this is where he flung himself on a heap of frozen orange flames of the *gulmohar* just to watch you get worried, this is where he sang... So you make a counter request. That *Maavshi* be allowed to accompany you, and that you be allowed to take a break on the way back.

The schoolchildren stay at Ganapatipule for a week, making short daily excursions. To Ratnagiri, the home of the *alphonso* mango; to Chiplun, where students are shown the temple dedicated to Lord Parshuram, the man who chopped off his mother's head to prove his obedience to his father and then went on to extract Konkan out of the sea; to Sindhudurg, the fort on a low rocky island off Malvan.

Many years after Ravindra and you stood at the mill-town beach, getting tickled between the toes by the receding water, the sea is flooding your senses.

The deserted beach and the presence of friends like Urmi and Ulka, allow your Aquarian blood to finally mingle with water. Once upon a time, a fearless boy called *Dada* took the plunge with you into a flooded river. Today, it is time for you to drag Urmi and Ulka and Manisha and all the boys and girls in your care, into the warm, sparkling clean, knee-deep waters.

This is where it all starts.

This is how it all starts.

Sea-water, womb water, blood.

Life, consciousness, love.

When you hear Manisha scream in delight, you gurgle in happiness. Ulka and Urmi stand on either side of you, as you float on your back, close your eyes and bob away with your senses. You are the warmth of the sun on the wetness of your face. You are the salt taste at the edge of your nostrils. You are the rude shove and tug of the waves on the body. You are the sound of a million fish conversations and twenty young boys and girls screaming on the beach.

You are pure awareness and eternal bliss.

After the excited kids go off to sleep that evening, Urmi, Ulka, *Maavshi* and you sit around a fire, the two 'U's with their arms around your shoulders. You take turns singing nonsensical songs, giggling and laughing like teenagers. You are drunk on togetherness. When one of the night guards appears out of nowhere, and demands to know where you are from, you let Urmi engage him with inanities, while you paint your face black with the ash – you learnt the trick from your *Dada* – slip behind him and *boo* loudly. The hapless man jumps out of his skin, and the night resounds with your combined laughter, scattered to the winds by the flames.

You wish Sandhya and Kausalya were here too, they would have loved this cocooned camaraderie. A sisterhood without name, sprung out of a criss-crossing of destinies.

A fatherless, motherless girl from a village, another who wore nail polish to the smelly loos of Maska Chawl, another born with a golden voice, and an old woman who accepted whatever life flung at her... *Maavshi* hums a song by Bahina*baai*, all the tragedy and heartbreak and optimism of life captured in a few folksy sentences by the genius of an illiterate but worldly-wise housewife.

Next morning, *Maavshi* and you get off at the crossroads. The children's goodbye is like ribbons of multicoloured screams as the bus pulls off. Urmi and Ulka, lulled into a delicious languor after a long time, wave as the bus proceeds to its last sector to Mahabaleshwar.

Maavshi and you stand there, at the crossroads between the past and future, at the road that forks off into Wada, the village that gave birth to you.

It has been seventeen years since you swore never to return.

Will the river still be hibernating in pools that expose their memories? Will *Dada*'s soul be waiting for you near the River Goddess' temple, so he can make you laugh and forget your anguish for your son? Will your home, your father's home, still have the creaking swing in its porch?

Was it right of you to travel so far away from your village, you authority-accosting, beer-swigging, husband-abandoning, new-men-adopting wench?

Why have you returned, when you swore to *Dada* you wouldn't?

What about *Bhai*? Will he want to greet you?

You did not ask *Bhai*'s permission before you did the unspeakable act of confronting a holy Brahmin, did you? You did not even attend his wedding, remember? You live separately from your husband, do not think your brother doesn't know. You never write letters to him, never send him a gift, never participate in his life.

Between him and his wife and his children playing in the courtyard (where one generation departed from, the other is gambolling and frolicking) and you, there are far too many unresolved issues.

He called you his only sister, but you never tried to understand him as your only surviving brother.

Despite sharing a womb, the distance between you has no bridge. Or so you think.

When he emerges out of the room of the gods, for a moment, your heart misses a beat.

Baba!

He has grown a beard like your father had. Peanut-butter skin stretched across hard plates of cheekbones, and life ploughing its furrows on the rest of his face.

Without thinking about it, you bend down to touch his feet. When you stand up, the two of you hug each other.

He sits on the teak swing, while *Maavshi* and you sit on two new wooden chairs.

He's never been good at conversation.

'Meera...!' he calls for his wife. A round-faced woman responds to his call, carrying two cups of tea and some glucose biscuits. The six-yard sari has migrated from city to village.

'You are in Bombay still...?'

'No, *Bhai*, I work in Mahabaleshwar... *Maavshi* stays with me... I'll write down the address...if you ever come there,' you add, scribbling the address on a chit of paper, a lame attempt to reduce his embarrassment, maybe he presumed you were already with another man.

'Why don't you stay tonight...I mean...as long as you want?'

'It's okay...school will start, the students will come... just wanted to see how everything was, the village was...'

You get up, do an awkward *namaskar*, then ask, 'Wanted to see my room...'

He gets off the swing and gestures towards the door.

There is much more light. The window is bigger, the vertical bars are gone. Outside, is the distant memory of

Dada, inside the memory of a tired mother. Both memories are dry and dusty, from another lifetime. You wait for the body to react, nothing happens.

'Okay...' you say, and thus ends the meeting between eldest brother and sister.

You struggle to find your way towards the river.

So much has changed.

The *paarijaat* tree stands flowerless, witness to a skirmish between a sorrow-crazed sister and a paralysed Brahmin.

The river lies in *rigor mortis* under the sky; intravenous tubes powered by pumps reach into her innards and suck out all the magic she ever possessed. Instead of pools covered with sheets of sunshine there are puddles of green pus, with flies settling on bits of dung.

You stand next to the temple of the River Goddess, a lone lamp battles the forces of change. You kneel down and touch the stone outside with your forehead. This is where your *Dada* was murdered: his cries were like a goat getting its throat slit.

You walk past the crematorium. It took her a long time to burn, because your mother carried a secret inside her, a secret too big to be consumed by the fire of wood.

You walk back to the highway, abandoning your paradise for the last time in your life.

Why did you return in the first place?

'I too want to close some chapters...like *Mai* did.'

❧ 32 ❧
Roman Circus

YOU RETURN TO THE SCHOOL with a deep sense of peace, only to discover it in turmoil. The teachers appear distracted. The younger students are their usual chirpy selves, but the older students are subdued, more clannish than usual, as if waiting for some resolution. The atmosphere is a fabric stretched so tight, even if you laughed out loud it would rip to shreds.

The December chill runs in veins, yet it's unable to quench the simmering discomfort. The anger comes out as steaming breath, hangs in the winter air.

You are not part of the teaching staff, so you are removed from the epicentre of this disturbance. A Class Twelve girl has become pregnant on campus. Unprecedented. There have been instances in 'other *nouveau riche* schools' but never in the bastion of values that is New Era. Mrs Luthra struggles with her response, shaken, diffident. She seeks support from all quarters. There is an emergency meeting of all staff at her bungalow, because the Teachers' Room is part of the school complex, and Mrs Luthra does not want the students to be exposed to what she believes will be an explosive meeting... All staff members, Desai, Kunte, Pardiwalla, Premji, Kamath, Mrs Sharma...teachers, housemasters, housemistresses, chief administrator... everybody sits staring at the floor.

'Her name is Shyamoli. The only daughter of a rich diamond merchant from Bombay. Her parents are politically well-connected. I have been waiting for this meeting...I have to inform him...but what to say...I want your help...'

Mrs Luthra's introduction to the culprit is over. Shyamoli has been staying at Gulmohar House, the hostel where senior girls stay under the watchful eye of Mrs Naik, the geography teacher. Mr Naik is the maths teacher, and the childless couple have been with the school for over twelve years. You had made friends with them during the first period of leave in the school.

'Mrs Naik, you wanted to say something...?'

Mrs Naik stares at the floor. Shrivelled, bespectacled, withdrawn. She sniffles. Everybody waits.

'I'm sorry, I failed, so many years as a housemistress, nothing like this...so shameful...I can't believe...I can't,' she blurts out. Mr Naik, her husband, holds her palm in his, presses it.

The silence has a mixed flavour. You taste anger and pity and sympathy.

'Probably you know if she was meeting someone secretly...not anybody from outside the school... otherwise we are dead...' Mr Pardiwalla is the first to express his fears.

After that, it is the art teacher, Mr Kunte's, turn to point a finger.

'That is not a secret, sir...Rajeev Mehrotra, Class Twelve also, from Jacaranda House... I am knowing, everybody is, I just am speaking on behalf of everybody, we are knowing their love since one year ago...even in physics experiment class, no, Desai, what...?'

You stare at your own fingers as the voices slowly build up, feeding on each other, tearing ripe morsels of flesh from a young girl's body, laughing at a young boy's wayward penis. It's a Roman Circus, where human beings watch human beings battle animals, and then vote to decide which victor would die, which victim would survive.

Between one of the uncomfortable pauses, you hear a voice ask a rather pertinent question.

'Has anybody spoken to Shyamoli and asked how...or why it happened?'

Many heartbeats later, you discover the voice is your own. You discover that some men and women are looking at you quizzically. Well, you are not exactly the seniormost person in the room, you have no executive powers, you are just a fixture in the School Welfare Committee.

'Want to try?' asks Mr Pardiwalla, and somebody snickers. One knife has swiftly been inserted between flesh and bone.

'Yes. I guess that would be the first step in deciding who is guilty, don't you think?' Somebody inside you has decided to don steel armour and plunge headlong into battle.

'If she has no sense of right or wrong, why bother? Is this what the school's values taught her? And will her parents believe us? Damn youngsters...just throw her out...' Mr Naik's quivering indignation sets a few heads nodding.

'Agreed. Can we at least find out if she has a sense of right or wrong? And perhaps her parents will believe her at least.' Who is speaking? You are on autopilot, the answers spring out of the art of seeing the other viewpoint. No, they also spring out of wanting to defend a woman.

'Perhaps, you are an expert in such affairs...' Mr Naik's voice is dipped in the same venom sacs that Krishna*rao* is equipped with. Human beings suppress thoughts, but they sprout their angry shoots the moment the soil is damp enough. Obviously Mr Naik has notions about you that are not charitable.

You do not reply. But yes, you are qualified. A man who tied a sacred thread around your neck banished you forever without trial. You know how it feels.

You hear another familiar voice. Urmi. One of the two 'U' sisters.

'What's wrong in speaking to Shyamoli? She is only a youngster...can't we as adults at least find out why she did what she did? It's not as if we are perfect.'

There is an uneasy hiatus.

Mrs Luthra steps in. 'Okay, if you don't mind, I would like Maya to speak to Shyamoli and give us...a...a report...'

The incident has divided the school. Male vs female. Teachers vs students. Teachers vs housemasters and mistresses. The battles are fought covertly. Acidic remarks spat out on unsuspecting faces. Sharp steely jibes flying behind turned backs. Sly knowing grins running their tongues along bodies.

In the library, some of the Class Twelve boys make you a target.

'Do you think the Chief Investigating Officer knows anything about pregnancy?' asks one boy loudly.

'Well, only her runaway husband can tell us...' replies another.

The laughter sends out a shower of razor blades towards you, slitting skin.

You will wait for the real gladiatorial combat to begin before you react to the thin enervating cuts all over your body.

You will titrate the pain, letting its drops drip on the fabric of the future; allow that pain to be your guide in understanding the scars on others. 'Wait,' you say to yourself, 'wait till you have heard her out.'

When you enter Gulmohar House that late evening, you don't know what to expect. All you know is you have to help Shyamoli.

White skirt and blouse, royal blue school cardigan, shoulder-length hair, long dignified face, dark circles under eyes. She appears calm. Until you lock the door of the room and she starts speaking.

'I want to leave this place as soon as I can, and if I am not allowed to speak to my father I am going to take you to court...'

She speaks in a controlled even tone, waits for you to react. You stare back.

'And who are you and why have you come here...to give me one more lecture about how I must protect the *izzat* of this school...?'

Even you did not know how well your past has prepared you for unforeseen events.

Instead of a seeing a hormone-crazed, rich spoilt girl cocking a snook at an establishment that's scurrying to cover its exposed backside, you see yourself. You smile at the memories.

Shyamoli walks up to you and snarls, 'Find it funny...want to feel what this problem feels like...bloody cheap housemistress?' She starts hitting her midriff.

You grab her hand.

'You are not the first woman to be blamed for things she has not done...'

Shyamoli will not hijack words as alibis. She has to hurt real people, let them bleed, and get them to reveal their true colours so she can find out if they are friends or foes.

She pushes your hand away, shouts, 'So...what can all you teachers do...fucking exploiters...'

You had decided you would stay calm. Yet you shout back out of your own pain. The crimson spreads inside your throat.

'Yes, you can be exploited...but not without your permission...understand...I know...I know...more than you will ever do...'

Shyamoli stares at you, grows quiet. You haven't given any indication of which side you are on. This is taking too long. She needs support. She has to end this.

It's clear she is as scared of her parents as she is of her teachers. Will she end up sending dried-blood-red rose petals to her brother?

She makes one last attempt to scare you.

'Listen, my father is one of the biggest diamond merchants in the world...he will buy off this school and all you middle-class...'

Your reply cuts her mid-sentence. 'Shyamoli, so is my brother...he too lives in Antwerp...' then you walk up to her, hold her hand and whisper, 'My child...this is not about how to hurt each other more...this is about hurting less... I told you I was only years older than you when something similar happened to me...except my baby was in my arms.'

Shyamoli is exhausted. Amazingly enough, the window has the same vertical bars your tiny room in Wada had. Universal symbol. Vertical lines mean a prison, whether painted on your face or held between brothers and sisters, or fake lovers and victims of love.

Outside, the moon has an unscheduled miscarriage. Ugly clots of silence get released. The air grows sticky.

'Shyamoli...' It's your turn to confide, 'I was your age when someone blamed me for something...you can either tell me or be bound by your own secret...'

She stares at the floor. The December cold swirls around the two of you, pushing you closer, making you breathe air mixed by each other's breath.

'But I love him...'

In how many ways must love betray love till it learns a lesson?

'Then he must take responsibility...is there love without responsibility...?'

'But he will be destroyed...he did not want to do it...I told him it was okay...I wanted him to be part of me...'

'And he did...and now he has to admit he is part of the problem...'

You are sitting next to her now. She holds your hand, but it is not out of newfound intimacy, it is just to reassure herself that it is a living human listening to her.

'Don't abandon me...wait...just wait...'

She buys time, while inside her one Shyamoli battles another. Clutch the hard nut of the secret, Shyamoli, if you let it fall the world might...will laugh at you, ridicule you... 'Shit, this is all it was...a dry berry, an ovary punctured by a wayward sperm...we've seen so many like these before...ha, ha...ha...'

'I can't...' she says, and lets go of your hand.

It is only during your third meeting, a meeting that doesn't take place in Gulmohar, because the place itself seems to spook Shyamoli, and it is only after she has genuinely realised the mess she is in that Shyamoli unburdens herself.

You do not know if Mrs Luthra will have the strength to act upon Shyamoli's confession.

You do not know if secluded universes with their own caucuses have any fairness and justice left.

But you have promised yourself you will not let Shyamoli suffer the way you did.

So you meet Mrs Luthra alone. You show her the proof, and make her promise you that she will do everything to be just and fair to the student.

After Mrs Luthra has given you her word, you 'give your report' at the next secret meeting of the school committee.

'It was not Rajeev Mehrotra who was responsible...but a teacher.'

'You actually have proof...?' an incredulous Mr Pardiwalla is the first to break the silence.

'How can this be?' says Mr Kunte.

'I have told Mrs Luthra who it was two days ago, and there is enough proof...my own submission is that we take her parents into confidence and explain the entire episode...and ask forgiveness...and...'

You have not expected this of yourself. But probably everything is coming together now.

'...I suggest we should definitely ask the teacher who caused this pain to Shyamoli to leave the school...she really believes she is in love. But I suggest we show the same compassion to the teacher that we demand towards Shyamoli. Age is no insurance against the ignorance of one's motives.'

'So what makes you so certain...?' asks Mr Naik, angry that his wife is somehow indicted in the whole affair.

You stare back at him until he lowers his gaze.

Maybe the loss of a son to music has made you fearless...now you have nothing to lose? Maybe you have given up on wanting to maintain an equation with a constantly false world. Maybe it's the simple fact that you know the truth now.

'I think we will all be happier if we let the culprit go away by himself...there is no need to have a public trial...'

'But Mrs Luthra...what is this...what happens to our tradition...you really want that nobody knows who the person was or what?' Clueless Mr Pardiwalla is at it again.

Mrs Luthra has had enough time to make up her mind.

'My decision has been made. I spoke to the Board Members over the past two days and got their permission to rusticate the teacher who got involved with Shyamoli.

But I will wait for one day more to allow the teacher to submit his resignation by himself. It will help him in his career, or whatever is left of it.

I have informed the parents that they need to come

here as soon as possible.

I have asked Dr Rastogi to stand by and advise Shyamoli and the parents the medical alternatives available for Shyamoli.

If the parents proceed legally, the school will not support the teacher...our laws on the matter are very clear.

I thank you all for being concerned and thank Maya for her effort in managing to get Shyamoli to confess...sorry, to tell us the truth.'

Clear, crisp certainty: there are no questions after that speech.

✈ 33 ✈
Three Faces and a Mask

MRS LUTHRA HAS invited you to dinner at her bungalow where she lives by herself, with just an old maidservant, Maina, for company. She wants to celebrate the end of Part One of the episode.

'What do you think the parents will do?'

'I don't know. But I think they will be less angry with the teacher and more angry with Shyamoli.'

Mrs Luthra pats your shoulder. 'You must talk about your past more often...it will lessen the pain.'

Were you still measuring the world the way you measured the ones closest to you? And is your mind such a glass house that Mrs Luthra can see the naked thoughts slithering about?

As you sit for dinner, there is a knock on the door.

It reminds you of the door opening when Ravindra came to meet you at Hari Niwas. The servant who opens the door seems to know that the person outside is a special person, someone who has, with heart-pounding effort, dragged a bundle of pain to Mrs Luthra's doorstep. The servant, Maina, doesn't ask Mrs Luthra's permission, she just holds the door open.

Once again, the roles are the same. The person outside the door has come with angry questions, you sit inside with known answers.

Mrs Naik stands before the two of you wrapped in a shawl.

'*Aaiye*!' Mrs Luthra welcomes her.

She resembles Shyamoli now, her smile stretched tight on the hooks of uncertainty.

'Mrs Luthra...'

Both of you wait for her to continue.

Maina hands over a glass of hot tea to Mrs Naik, then melts into the shadows of the kitchen, trained not to listen to the secrets revealed in the school Principal's home.

'Who is the person...the teacher...at least I must be told...how is it possible...?'

Mrs Luthra looks at you, then nods, as if to say, 'You take this answer.'

'Mrs Naik, remember you went off to meet your mother, she was ailing, or something, during the November holidays?' You don't want to hurt her because you know how it feels.

She nods.

Then clutches at a straw, blurts out. 'But Mrs Sharma was standing in for me...so she must be held responsible...' Then she flares, '...even you have gone off so many times for your son's programmes...how come Mrs Luthra allowed you...and that old woman, *Maavshi* was looking after your wards...'

You ignore the attack. It's the natural reaction of a trapped mind.

'You remember your husband did not accompany you

217

and some of the girls in the hostel, including Shyamoli, were here for a week, waiting for their parents or guardians...?'

She stands up and moves towards the two of you at the dinner table.

'Are you saying, Keshu, I mean, Mr Naik allowed somebody to actually come to the Gulmohar House and...do that thing to Shyamoli...no, he wouldn't!'

You stare at the table. This is so demeaning. 'I know how you feel, because I have been through this.'

Despite the fear that she is going to grow violent against you, you get up and put your arm around her shoulder and make her sit on the sofa again. Then you kneel next to her. Time to end this charade.

'Mr Naik was giving Shyamoli maths tutorials. She had improved dramatically because of them. She felt he was doing it especially for her. We don't know what his need was...her need as an adolescent was clear...she was experiencing the first love in her life...she wanted to experience everything associated with it...he fought the temptation...but it ended up like this...'

'No!' she screams, '...don't tell me such dirty lies, how can you, just because your husband abandoned you...?' She pushes you, you fall on your backside, the same backside that bore the pain of a father-in-law's ire.

Inside you, there is a quiet explosion of anger. What the hell does she know about your husband? Then you calm down. It is precisely because she doesn't know that she has reached that conclusion.

So you go up to Mrs Luthra and ask her to bring out the letters. Mrs Luthra has created copies of the letter (that's how she has survived the politics of this golden cage), so that no court, no jury can destroy the originals.

Once, a single letter from Paris had changed how your own destiny would be spelt out. Now the letters between Mr Naik and Shyamoli are doing the same. Earlier, four lives were involved: Ravi, Sharan, *Nana* and you. This time, many more await a resolution: a childless couple, an attractive adolescent girl, a wrongly accused boy, a gaggle of teachers who had, for too long, lived in a sheltered environment, perhaps regressing into adolescence themselves...

Mrs Naik does not weep. (You must learn this art from her.) She stares at the letters, hands them back to Mrs Luthra, turns and marches off in the heartless black cold of Mahabaleshwar. You don't even want to imagine what is passing through her mind. Her own image of herself as a conscientious housemistress and dutiful companion destroyed by her husband's lure of plump flesh and young love. It reminds you of a painting done by Ravindra: one lady kisses a man passionately, not aware that it is a mask tied at the back of his head, while the man kisses another woman.

Three faces and a mask.

The school holds its collective breath for a dramatic *denouement*, nothing visibly dramatic really happens.

Mrs Luthra is able to end all talk with quiet efficiency. Mr Naik's resignation arrives at her desk mysteriously. The Naiks leave in the middle of the night. The notice on the Teacher's Room softboard, signed by Mrs Luthra, announces that the 'Mr and Mrs Naik have resigned, and the new housemistress of Gulmohar House is a Marathi teacher, Urmi Sawant. The school administration has identified candidates for a new maths and geography teacher and their appointments will be finalised soon.'

Shyamoli's parents arrive, listen to Mrs Luthra and to you, glance at the letters, and leave with Shyamoli. You request them to be kind to their daughter, but they do not respond. The father is tight-jawed; he writes a request to Mrs Luthra to withdraw his daughter from New Era School with 'immediate effect'. Just before he leaves, he tells Mrs Luthra that she will be hearing from the Board soon. Mrs Luthra doesn't flinch.

You get just one opportunity to hug Shyamoli, and you whisper, 'There are many forms of love, Shyamoli, you just need to work it out for yourself.'

Like her parents, she does not respond either.

❧ 34 ❧

Not Without Your Permission

SCHOOL RETURNS to its former quietude, but you do not understand the full import of the emotions within you. You seem to want to shut every single book of life, like *Mai* was doing when she was ill, preparing for her death.

You want to leave no obligations unfulfilled, no hungers unfed.

You insist on buying gifts for Pankaj when you meet him during the winter holidays in Bombay. You buy books for Varun, for Sylvia and Mahadevan, for Mrs Shah, for Mr Ganguly. Everything feels peaceful, but hollow.

You can no longer suppress the desire to see Sharan. That is one page of your life that keeps fluttering, demanding to be read.

'If the guru's discipline does not allow Sharan to even meet those nearest to him, well, a mother can always find a way out.'

You go back to scanning newspapers. That was the way you found this damned gilded cage anyway. The opportunity presents itself a couple of years later at an Emerging Artistes' Festival during Ganesh Chaturthi in Poona. All those who will perform are sons of known gurus.

Sharan will be the only exception.

Poona is close enough (it will take you five hours). You can travel by bus, attend the festival and return by morning. Nobody would know.

The hall is packed with classical music *aficionados*. You lower yourself gingerly on a wooden chair with a Rexine centre in the last row, conscious of the rustle of your very old silk sari. You pulled it out last when you went for the Marathi Literary Sammelan in Nagpur.

'Sharan Patil, the youngest performer today!'

The applause after the announcement is deafening.

Then silence.

Someone coughs as Sharan enters.

His father's cheeks, his mother's eyes.

'Oh God, my baby's grown so tall, so thin. (Actually, he is quite muscular, it's only in your eyes he appears thin.) Does he not eat enough? What does that accursed Pandit*ji* feed him? Why did I not send him the snacks that *Maavshi* makes for the hostel kids, why did I not ask permission...'

Sharan salutes the audience with a polite *namaskaar*, squats cross-legged on the white mattress, touches his ear to show his respect for his guru, then jerks you out of your uncharacteristic and incessant mental babbling by calling out to you.

'*Aai, aadnya.*'

'Mother, I seek your permission.'

You jump up, smile, and are about to walk towards the stage.

'How did he know? Nobody knows I am here!'

The stage lights are on him, so your son cannot see your half-hearted leap.

But that voice clear as a stone hitting a metal bell on a wintry morning stops you.

You realise that Sharan starts all his recitals by paying his respects to you.

'Dear friends, this is my first public recital after having had the honour of being accepted as a disciple by my guru*ji*, Pandit Arolikar. To him I shall be eternally grateful. But please indulge me and allow me to speak for a couple of minutes. Because I need to thank others who made this journey possible. You know...most human beings have only one father, and one mother. I have been fortunate to have more than one. A father who conceived me and a father who gave birth to the music in me. A mother who gave birth to me, and music, which has been my mother for the past ten years.

'Before I begin the actual recital, with the permission of this august audience and my guru*ji*, I'd like to sing a song that I learnt while I was a baby. My mother sang it for me...because her father sang it for her.'

You return to your seat and sit down, your heart still hammering, creating tiny echoes in the hollow cups of your *mangalsutra*.

The woman next to you smiles wanly.

'One day I will discover the true meaning of this *shloka*...maybe that day I will be able to stop singing...and return to listening to my senses like my mother taught me.'

He smiles to himself, then continues.

'You will not believe it, but my mother taught me to

recognise a tree by touching its bark blindfolded, to listen to stars on cold nights, she probably taught me the sound of the universe in her womb...'

The applause seems never ending.

All the yearning of all the years explodes inside you. 'My prince...my baby...he has not forgotten me...he will not forget me...'

You abandon control. You stuff the *pallu* of your sari into your mouth to choke a sob, like your mother did, when your father left home in his pursuit of light. You taste metal and memory and helplessness and joy.

Then Sharan proves his musical education was perfect by twisting fibres of sunlight and nostalgia into the sound of your favourite song.

'Manobuddhi ahankaar chittaani...'

The sound of the universe is being explained to the audience: hurricanes wink inside it, the furnace of a million suns is quenched, relationships are exposed belly-up, half-truth is annihilated.

The woman sitting next to you thinks your tears are your joyous reaction to the singer's spellbinding voice, as it leaps off peaks, lands silkily unhurt, takes off again.

Maybe he had understood the meaning of the *shloka* before you did. It does not matter anymore: the audience is ecstatic about Sharan's singing.

The scars on your heart were worth his success.

The bus ride through the night back to Mahabaleshwar is the opposite of the bus ride through the night you undertook many years ago from Bombay to Wada: instead of your *Dada*'s pleading face, Sharan's quiet visage intersects the dreams under your sandpaper-slivered eyelids.

᠊ᠥ 35 ᠊ᠥ
Surrender

A COUPLE OF YEARS LATER, as you doze in your room on a Sunday, letting your mind float, there is a knock on the open door. It is the *darwaan*, he has returned with his temple shaped hat, and, like many years ago, with Ravindra.

You push yourself off the chair with your left hand while your right hand adjusts your *pallu*, you never quite got it right, always a balloon of starched cotton around your sacral region.

Ravindra.

Can't be.

He must be in Paris with Christine, at least that's what you believe would have been the right thing for him to do, and anyway, he's much older. You are dreaming a vivid dream of course, of the type Freud mentions so often, almost projected in space, a Lothar-Diana-Mandrake comic book parapsychology trick.

Ravindra, younger, slightly thicker lips, no pockmarks. Late afternoon sleep at the edge of a fubsy pigeon's stream of cooing and gurgling always leads to hallucinations.

Ravindra, half-smiling, half-hesitant.

Then he loses his control and hugs you so hard you can't breathe.

'*Aai*!'

You believed you'd visited all the dark pools of memory during those long empty afternoons at the school while the flies drilled haphazard holes in the silence with their buzzsaws.

The pools were dry, exposing empty cages made of ribs hurt by brooms.

That is what you believed.

Why then are you biting your lower lip, trying to smother the sob of joy that is growing inside?

The Third Order of Love, Parent and Child.

You sit side by side on the only settee in your room, then you move your hand to cover his, but he extracts it, moves closer and hesitantly puts it around your bony back wrapped in a thin cotton blouse. His fingers will detect no bra strap, your triumphant city acquisition. You stopped wearing them when you stopped bothering about your appearance. He is taller than you, so he can see the grey in your hair.

In turn, your fingers feel the muscles in his arms, like cords twisted out of smooth solid wood.

His voice is heavy with guilt.

'*Aai*, you look so...frail. You have not been looking after yourself.'

You do not speak. It is enough that he has returned. That he did not throw you out of a home at midnight. That he did not accuse you of philandering.

Most important, that he wanted to sing so he could feel the harmony of the universe. Not for the hired love of a woman, or for the kiss of blowzy fame.

You rest your head on his shoulder. 'Thank you, River Goddess, so many departed, but someone returned.'

'*Aai*, look, you have one more very important guest.' His voice breaks you out of your reverie.

You look up and see Pandit Arolikar standing at the doorway, and behind him is Mr Bhatkhande. He is thinner now; the flesh hangs a bit around his jowls. But the moustache and the eyes that look within and without simultaneously have remained unchanged. You get up and bend down to touch Pandit*ji*'s feet.

He stops you mid-way, holds you by your shoulders.

'*Arre*, my child, don't do this. Do you know why I have come? I rarely leave Indore except for a couple of concerts every year, but somehow this time, I felt I owed it to you and to Kaivalya. I know it was hard for you to endure this test that I created. It is not just Sharan who has learnt that music is a demanding mistress, so have you.'

You whisper, 'Thank you' and rush into the kitchen to get something to welcome them with. *Maavshi* rushes in with you, truly excited. Her grandson is back too!

Sharan follows the two of you, and touches *Maavshi*'s feet. She hugs him, mutters, 'My *sona*, if you grow any bigger, I will not be able to put my arms around you,' then deflects her joy to you, 'Your *Aai* has waited for this moment for god knows how many years...'

You have a quiet dinner in Sharan's honour with Mr Bhatkhande, Bhivaji, Khot, Urmi and Ulka, and of course, Kausalya.

It is full moon night, and it is only natural that the guests insist on listening to Sharan's deep voice. All of you sit at the feet of the *gulmohar* overlooking the valley.

Sharan asks Pandit*ji*'s permission. 'Guru*ji*, what shall I sing?'

Pandit*ji* laughs. Thankfully, the valley is big enough to contain that condensed thunder.

'Do you think I did not see you writing those letters to your *Aai*, hiding under your blanket late at night?' Sharan smiles an embarrassed smile. His guru was indeed a *shataavadhaani*. 'Now why don't you show your old mother what your new mother taught you? Can you show her your love without words? After all you spent years learning this new language. Come on *beta*, show her what you can do…make your separation worth it.'

'*Malkauns*? It is late enough in the night.'

Both Pandit*ji* and Mr Bhatkhande nod at his choice. 'And *Malkauns* once represented love in the face of separation,' adds Pandit*ji*.

The group falls silent. A black canopy studded with stars waits to listen to the pure sound that conceived the universe. A tree with a strange name (the label you created hangs around its knees, '*Gulmohar*' and '*Delonix regia*') is witness to departures and arrivals. This is where Mr Bhatkhande requested you to let Sharan choose his path, this is where you discover that the choice was right.

Even you are surprised at the level of his '*tayyari*'. Sharan's singing is full of silver and diamonds and a waterfall roar. He unfolds the solemn meaning of the *raga*. Graceful oscillations and slow *glissandos* are technicalities you do not understand, but you can feel the love and separation.

You notice tears of joy streaming down Kausalya's cheeks. Mr Bhatkhande has buried his face in his hands…his guess was right.

On both counts.

Sharan is a magnificent 'creature of silence'. And his *gurubandhu*, Pandit Arolikar, has done an equally magnificent job of training him. And he has trained him in the true tradition of Indore: his soul sings for itself. If you are ready, you feel the resonance in your soul too.

This is not music; it is a conversation between Spirit and Spirit.

When the singing ends, nobody wants to move. But Urmi, Ulka, Bhivaji and Khot have to, they have early morning appointments: they bow respectfully to Pandit*ji* and leave.

Pandit*ji* looks at his friend, sighs and says something that startles you, 'Kaivalya, you sang like this on the day Sohini left, remember? Especially the opening *vilambit*...' he stops mid-sentence when he notices Mr Bhatkhande staring at you over Pandit*ji*'s shoulders.

Pandit*ji* turns to you, and asks softly, 'So he never told you about her...?'

You shake your head.

It's Mr Bhatkhande's turn to speak. 'You asked me once, Maya, under this very tree if I remember, whether I allowed everybody in my life to choose... Sohini was my wife, and she believed she had to end family life...I mean *grihasthashram*...to pursue her interest in singing...all three of us used to learn under the same guru... I took up this job, not strong enough to abandon my little Kausalya to music...it's a very old story...I don't know why Trimbak thought of her now...'

His voice has no emotion. But you notice Kausalya wrapping his fingers in hers, patting the ageing skin of his palm.

Pandit*ji*'s voice is even softer. 'Because I met her in Benaras when we went there for the Sankat Mochan festival...so did this lucky boy of yours...' Sharan stiffens. So do you. You remember Sharan's last letter. The lady who had met him after his recital.

'She too performed...I cannot describe that sound, Kaivalya...exactly like our guru*ji* predicted. It was appropriate that it all happened in Benaras...where Lord Shiva started the universe through sound... She sat there wearing white, her hair is white too, and to listen to her at dawn...'

Mr Bhatkhande smiles, cuddles Kausalya and kisses her hair. 'She found what she was looking for, *haan*, Kausalya, she found it.'

'Pandit*ji*, I have a small request.'

Everybody turns to you.

'I understand so little of the beauty of music, but I understand words...and the best words I have ever heard have been those sung by *Maavshi*.'

The three men smile. Kausalya has heard *Maavshi* before. She eggs her on. *Maavshi* refuses. She is too shy. Then Sharan goes to her, hugs her, whispers something in her ear, and drags her to the *gulmohar* platform.

She sits staring at the earth, and starts singing the same songs she sang on the beach in Ganapatipule.

> '*Life, dear life,*
> *Like hot pan on fire*
> *First angry singes on skin*
> *Then the bread...for kith and kin.*'

It's an untrained voice, except it is the antithesis of

230

Sohini's warning to Sharan.

Its beauty is the depth of its emotion.

Amor fati: love of one's fate. Every moment splits into two, and we have to decide to breathe life into one of two diverse long-chain polymers of probability. Choose the wrong one, you are responsible. Choose the right one, you are responsible again.

Kausalya made her choice, her mother made hers, Mr Bhatkhande made his, Ravindra made his, your father, *Maavshi* too...

What is and what can be, decide now, Maya.

As Sharan's voice once again caresses the moonbeams and returns, a voice inside you grows stronger.

This is it. This is the moment you must let go, Maya.

Sharan. Surrender.

Your son's name tells you what you must do.

You chose it eighteen years ago, as if to remind you of your responsibility in the future.

Surrender.

Surrender, Maya, to this great river of life.

Remember the chain of events your father unleashed when the teeth of attachment snapped shut around his ankles.

Surrender, since you will not be able to change a millisecond of anybody else's destiny.

Surrender, let him go, let him pursue his path to eternal bliss.

Remember what Christine, a stranger with blonde hair and a lover's heart, asked?

Remember why you answered with silence?

If you understand what you are, neither mother nor sister nor wife nor daughter...let him go. Else you spark off the same chain of events your father did.

If you already know that when love contains an 'I', it is misspelt and is therefore false love, let him go.

One moment, the pain is a thorn in your heart, the next moment it is a hole of light.

Inside you, a seed splits open the transparent integument surrounding it, reaches out to the sky with two luscious green flames of tender leaves.

That's right. The final frontier is your own attachment: to your children, your love, your idea of yourself.

And the only trick in the book is to break that attachment. Baba had done that vis-a-vis you, that's how your name vanished from the pages of his life.

And you have to do it now vis a vis Sharan.

☙ 36 ❧

The Valley of Confessions

WHILE YOU HAVE STRUGGLED with your thoughts, Mr Bhatkhande has gotten up and hugged Sharan. As he attempts to hug Pandit*ji*, Pandit*ji* roars, '*Haan*, this will not do *gurubandhu*...we cannot celebrate this moment by hugging each other like women...hope you have arranged for my favourite red-blooded female to enjoy the night...' he winks at Kausalya, who instead of being embarrassed, giggles.

Maavshi and you are still grappling with his shocking innuendo, while Kausalya has marched off to the Bhatkhande residence and returned with something wrapped in a brown paper bag. A bottle of Red Label whisky. Obviously, Mr Bhatkhande and Kausalya had known that Pandit*ji* and Sharan were arriving from Indore. Obviously, Mr Bhatkhande has found ways and means of procuring his *gurubandhu's* favourite tipple.

Mr Bhatkhande says with a straight face, 'That's an old music teacher's monthly salary you are drinking, *Padmashri* Arolikar...'

Pandit Arolikar, 'Yes, but it this old music teacher's

entire lifetime that was poured down your so-called grandson's throat...what is the price of that...tell me, you old bandicoot...*haan*?'

The banter and bonhomie reminds you of the parties in Hari Niwas. It is as if human beings are only separated physically, inside them they are one.

'Come on, let's show Lord Shiva what we feel about him...!' roars Pandit*ji*, downing a peg of whisky neat, 'Now that Sharan has joined his gang of mendicants!'

He makes Mr Bhatkhande and Sharan and Kausalya sit on either side of him, all of them legs folded, backs straight, eyes on the horizon, and says, 'Sohini!'

Both Mr Bhatkhande and Kausalya stare at him quizzically, and an animated Pandit*ji* slaps his thigh, roars, '*Arre,* I'm talking about *raag* Sohini...look at the time...what else can we sing...? It's three in the morning...'

You understand nothing. Why should he insist on only one *raag*? Some day, Mr Bhatkhande will explain how specific *raags* can be sung only at specific times of the day, it is something to do with the effect of musical notes on the human body.

It is a performance that the rest of India would have died for, and the select front-row audience consists of only two, *Maavshi* and you.

Pandit*ji* makes a severe dent in the level of liquid in the Red Label bottle even as he sings, he has decided this is a night to celebrate reunions.

Even to your untrained ears, it becomes clear that two voices out of four are sturdier and more flexible.

Neither Kausalya nor Mr Bhatkhande have engaged in the gruelling eight-hour schedules that the other two have maintained.

It is almost dawn. Pandit*ji* insists that he and Sharan now sing *raag* Bhairav. Bhairav, Lord Shiva. 'Let's wake him up...I'm sure he won't mind,' says Pandit*ji*.

It's an amphitheatre of the magnificent.

Would Ravindra be able to paint this moment?

The enormous flag of a pale blue sky burnt crisp chrome at its edges being unfurled by three ebony giants and one lilac female.

Would Krishna*rao* be able to condense this moment into a *haiku*?

> *'Blood within is blood without,*
> *Singing together*
> *The dawn of a joyous shout.'*

When the world's most powerful classical music concert ends, you are speechless.

But the older men in your life have much to say. The time for silence is over.

It's Mr Bhatkhande's turn first.

'You know Maya, how scared I was when I first recommended we take Sharan to Trimbak? I wasn't scared of what would happen because I understood Sharan's talent and Trimbak...but I was scared of my own guilt...I had retreated to a safer career for the sake of my daughter...and here I was, blithely recommending that you abandon your son to music...but...all's well that ends well.'

To your amazement, this is followed by Pandit*ji* himself.

'I had given both of you a fifty-fifty chance. I was certain a boy without a father would break down, or a mother without a son would... But now that you have seen what Sharan is capable of...I'm going to take him away again...from now on he'll concentrate on singing for himself...to discover himself...in the Indore *gharana* it's called singing for your soul...and now you can meet him whenever your heart feels like it...'

Little does either of them know what your heart has been through. You have jumped across the chasm.

When Sharan is ready to depart the next morning, you have no tears.

You smile at him, hug him, kiss his forehead, tell him next time you want to see your daughter-in-law, and please take care with the food, remember our first trip out of here to Kolhapur, when your stomach went on a non-co-operation movement.

He laughs an embarrassed laugh.

Pandit*ji* hugs you.

'They say in Indore *gharana*, the music guru and the spiritual guru are one. You know what, you brave little girl? I think you played that role for our Sharan over here. Be happy now, your world is neatly folded up for you.'

⮞ 37 ⮜
Halfway There

IT'S MRS LUTHRA who changes the equation. The equation between your inside and outside.

She accosts you in her usual put-on aggression.

'Maya, you are so sure of yourself inside you, so why do you act so unsure...why do you refuse to accept your own strengths?'

'What strengths?'

'The fact that you use your experience to learn about other human beings as well as yourself...why not accept that you can influence others? How long will you deny yourself your own life?'

You have never thought about yourself that way, despite Ravindra's letters, despite Sharan's letters...

'So what would you have me do?'

'I want to appoint you Senior Administrator of the school as well as Director of Personal Development... Old Mr Banerjee is about to retire...I feel you will change the school. I feel you will really make a difference here.'

So be it.

The first change that strikes you is that there is a

considerable change in your salary. You put away three-fourths of it in a bank against Sharan's name.

The second change is that you are free from the responsibilities of being a housemistress. You will miss managing the lovable brats in Laburnum House, but you will enjoy greater responsibility.

'Congrats, Maya, village girl. Welcome to the big league. No qualifications, no certificates, and yet you earn more than your father-in-law ever earned in his life, almost as much as Sanjay earns working in a bank.'

It makes you feel so proud, you drag *Maavshi* away from school on a holiday to Panhala, the fort next to Mahabaleshwar. You stay in a quaint old hotel, for the first time, you do not carry the burden of worrying about money.

The two of you sit under a blue sky while moonlight slithers off the white skin of eucalyptus trees heavy with deep green leaves.

'*Maavshi*, I don't know if you remember, but you said once that you were sure that I would look after my children because I had the strength of a man and a woman...that has happened...hasn't it?'

Maavshi reaches out and touches your face.

'My *sona*, you have looked after Sharan and many others you don't know...I never told you how much peace you brought into Pankaj's life...he was so close to his sister...and he promised me he would never lose you like he lost her...he was way too young then...and what about me? You decided without asking me that I become your child's grandmother...and I wondered...you know so much and you can do so much...but you never had questions about me...'

'*Maavshi*, it's over now...you and I and Sharan and Pankaj are free...we have to celebrate...you have been my mother...how do we celebrate this moment?'

'How would your mother do it?'

'I don't know...she never asked for anything...but I want to listen to your Bahina*baai* songs...and then we will sit and listen to what the moon and the trees have to say...and then, we will ask for nothing more from the universe...'

So the two of you sit, battle-hardy sisters, one who has survived the loss of parents and husband and sisters and sons and the other who is fortunate enough to have her son still alive...and *Maavshi* sings and you listen.

It's a new life.

You return charged up. This is it. Now you are no longer dependent on external relationships. Now everything you do is your own.

So be it.

The first change you insist on is change in the food served to the children. *Maavshi* and you conspire to recreate on a mass scale all the delicacies you knew. You force the kitchen manager to change the diet every day, to the delight of the children. Sundays bring special treats, however complex the preparation. The school cannot believe itself. In its history, it hasn't been served pancakes steamed in fragrant turmeric leaves. Lunches have never ended with *laddoos* made of *boondi*. Breakfasts have never included scrumptious *idlis* and *chutney*. All that was cold and clinical in food is replaced with all that is soul-warming and tasty.

The second change that comes about is in the library. You convince Mrs Luthra that more than textbooks, children need books. You ask the language teachers to recommend their list, and soon, the library has swollen. No longer is it packed with *Hardy Boys* and *Five Find-Outers*, it now boasts the best that all languages have to offer.

Mrs Luthra is concerned. 'Maya, who will read Sanskrit texts? This is madness.'

You argue. 'If you do not offer the taste of the highest that human beings have defined, how would the school live up to its name...this is a new era, this is a new world...everything has to be open, available, and then let the child decide what he or she is interested in...'

And then you push through a unique concept. No school has it. You create, with the help of Kausalya, a music library. Let the students soak sound for its own sake. Whether it is the tinkle of Mozart or the sweetness of Subbulakshmi, let the students come, sit in closed cubicles and listen to what they want to.

Some teachers put up a token fight, but you defeat them with rational logical arguments.

'Hello, Maya, rider of Shankar the buffalo, user of cowdung ash for brushing your teeth, woman who did not bathe naked for the first thirty years of your life...welcome to this new station. Happy to have you here...without a single talent to speak of.'

❧ 38 ❧
Shivoham, Shivoham

MAAVSHI WATCHES IN FASCINATION as your eyes begin to reflect what is happening in your consciousness.

They are no longer pools of mystery. Their depths are now transparent, and still. After the day's hustle and bustle, you sit by yourself under the *gulmohar*, the *shloka* resonating inside you.

You become a flame, attracting surprising moths to the light and the warmth.

Like Mrs Luthra. Her bravado as a grown-up woman is no different from that of the testosterone-afflicted adolescents in Class Twelve. She opens up to you, sniffles during one private dinner, explains the roots of her hardness, her domineering father, her cowering mother, her creation of a protective carapace. Others fly towards you through letters and confidential whispers. *Bhai*, Mrs Shah, Sylvia and Sanjay keep in touch; and your dear friend Pankaj, he finds peace and a home at last:

'Dearest Mayadidi,
Received your beautifully written letter. I personally

*believe we were all bit players in your life. You could
have sat licking your wounds in Maska Chawl, instead
you stepped out and discovered your own destiny...to
lead the young ones through their rightful education –
the role is perfect for you! There is much that you can
teach people...*

*My father passed away in his sleep last week. We flew
down to Bombay for his last rites. I did not inform you
because I had to return to Belgium almost immediately
after the ceremony.*

*Varun was there. I have decided to ask him to move
here with me: in this country our relationship does not
have to be hidden behind cloaks. It will be accepted as
naturally as you accepted it.*

I think we will plan our next party here! Imagine!

*Congratulations on Sharan's awesome success...you
deserve it as much as he...not everybody runs away, na,
didi?*

*With lots of love and pride,
Pankaj.'*

And finally, another surprise from Bombay. An irregular
adolescent voice; the lower octaves heavy with pain.

*'Dear Mrs Patil,
How do I begin?
It's been two years since I left New Era.
I went with my Dad to Europe and they used the
phrase 'medical termination of pregnancy' for what they
did to me there. Those were horrible days, but it does
not pain me so much inside my heart now. I am in*

Bombay now.

When sometimes at night I lie under the blanket, I think about everything and I say to myself there was one person who I looked down upon and insulted but it was she who helped me. I never thanked you properly. I want to do so now.

Some of my friends write to me and they tell me how many interesting things you know. Maybe you will pardon my silly reactions then, and write to me. Maybe I will learn from you how to use my own hurt to understand others less fortunate.

Will you write please...you could be the friend I can trust, you know?

Yours,

Shyamoli.'

As you read the letters you float on an ocean of peace.

The waves are events, but you know that under those disturbances, the water remains unchanged.

Psychologists say that your dreams are the mirror of your subconscious.

Mystics say they are the mirror of all consciousness.

One night, all the men in your life come to you.

Not just Sharan but Krishna*rao* and Ravindra and Pankaj and *Dada* and *Bhai* and Sanjay and Pandit*ji* too. They ceremoniously untie the masks off their faces, and lie down to sleep next to you: relieved that you appear to know when they should wake up and get on with their performances.

You feel you have the knowledge of a goddess, you remember the secrets of the universe, you can see the

243

truth behind delusion.

The curtains have come down on yet another act. You pat their heads affectionately, whispering wordlessly in your dreams.

'Unlike me, unlike us ordinary people, you were born with such talent it could dispel darkness, first in your own life, and then in the lives of others. You warriors of light...'

But you stop talking because they mutely stare back. Somehow they have sensed that you are beginning to understand something about life that is much larger than their talent. You smile back, wanting to hold them all to your heart.

'I? What have I understood except the meaning of a centuries-old song? What have I experienced? It is nothing... This taste of infinity, anybody can have it! Anybody...'

A thunderclap snaps you out of your dream.

It is dawn, time to greet newness. You feel extraordinarily light and clear-headed. You walk out of the hostel, walk towards the valley, and stand at the edge of the cliff, gulping fresh air.

Below you, a new world is being born.

Imagine, Maya! For decades the names of the relationships had you fooled: brother, husband, poet, friend, son. You could not have changed one hair's breadth of their destiny.

They became the human beings they most desired to be, despite their talent.

You are free to be the human being you most desire to be despite your *lack* of talent.

No ambition, no fear, no anger, no desires, no

disappointments, no lust, no jealousy…no attachment to the memory of a husband.

As if to confirm all of this to yourself, you take off your *mangalsutra* and bury it under the *gulmohar*.

And, finally, no attachments even to the belated fruit of your womb, your son. You bring out the envelope of capillaries, with all those beautiful letters and set them on fire.

It is your offering to the five *mahabhutaas*, to the warp and weft of the universe your father attempted to unravel.

Light flares across the sky and inside you.

When the little girl under the *paarijaat* chanted, '*Chidanandarupah shivoham, shivoham,*' when she promised her father that she would be happy without anybody, she did not know what she meant, but she had been right – for thirty long years…

Many thousand voices inside you, past and future, join the chant of the universe.

'*Manobuddhi ahankaar chittani naaham…*'

As the breeze picks up, you raise your arms to embrace everybody and everything, to dissolve boundaries, to fly.

Then, for the first time in your life, when the rain comes, it brings not the pain of separation, but sweet deliverance, grace and benediction.

Maya is the name of the twin-headed woman who waylays seekers of truth. Maya is the goddess who creates illusion by creating divisions.

But this Maya is now whole within herself.

Time to go back and practise your delectable art of living.

❧ Glossary ❦

The *Shloka* or chant that forms the leit motif is Shankaracharya's *Atma Shatakam*, or Six Verses about the Self. Each of the verses is immediately followed by its English translation within the main body of the book.

The Indian Constitution recognises eighteen languages; there are over 1600 dialects in India. Most of the words below are common to more than one language, specifically Sanskrit, Hindi, Marathi, and Urdu. Indians who think, write or speak in other languages may or may not be familiar with these words.

Aadnya: Permission; I seek your permission.
Aai: Mother.
Aaiye: 'Please come in' (Respectful).
Aashirwaad: Blessings.
Abhang: Literally, 'that which cannot be split'. Here it refers to the poetic form adopted by the Marathi poet-saints, notably Sant Namdeo and Sant Tukaram.
Aghora: The Left Hand Path ('*Vama Marga*') of Illumination/Liberation, as opposed to Right Hand Path (*Dakshina Marg*). The *Dakshina Marg* is recommended for those who seek steady progress with minimum risks, the other is a 'high-risk, high-gain' path.
Aghori: One who practices the Left Hand Path of Illumination.
Ajji: Grandmother.
Alphonso: Variety of mango, allegedly the finest in India; grown exclusively in a district of the Konkan (West) coast of India.
Arre: 'Hey'.

Ashoka: Botanically, '*Saraca asoca*'. One of the five sacred trees in Hinduism. Lord Buddha was born under an '*Ashoka*' tree, hence it is sacred for Buddhists as well.

Baba, also *Baabaa*: Father. There is a theory that in India, most combinations of a consonant and the doubled vowel 'aa' refers to a specific relationship. Thus, '*Maamaa*' is mother's brother, *Chaachaa* and *Kaakaa* is father's brother, *Daadaa* is elder brother or grandfather...and so on.

Bahinabaai: Illiterate poet from Maharashtra (1880-1951), who composed and sang her poems. They were written down by her son, who remembered them. One of the most memorable collections of poems in Marathi literature.

Baithakh: Sit-ups.

Bandish: A musical composition fixed in a rhythmic pattern; part of a *raga*.

Beedi: Indigenous cigarette made by rolling tobacco in tobacco leaves.

Besan: Chickpea flour.

Besan laddoos: A sweet made with chickpea flour and clarified butter, and rolled into balls.

Beta: Literally, 'son'; also affectionately 'child'.

Bhenchod: Literally, 'Sister-fucker'.

Bhai, also *Dada*: Term of respect, used for an older brother.

Bhakti: Devotion; devotional. One of the four ways of pursuit of the ultimate according to your psychosomatic constitution. Those driven by rational-analytical thought adopt the *Dnyana* (Knowledge) *Marg* (path); those driven by their hearts follow the *Bhakti* (Devotion) *Marg*; those driven by action adopt the *Karma* (Action) *Marg*.

Bhel: A savoury dish consisting of a mixture of various

chutneys puffed rice and whole-wheat chips. Eaten with diced tomatoes, onions and green chillies.

Bhootbaaji: Dabbling in the occult. (*Bhoot*: ghost; *baaji*: practice of).

Bindi: Sticker dot (or painted on with kohl/kumkum) worn by women, on centre-forehead, between the eyes. Either used as a symbol of marriage, or to beautify the face.

Boondi: Lentil balls made from chickpea flour and spices.

Brahmin: One of the four principal castes in Indian society, originally based on functions. The function of the Brahmin was to pursue the knowledge of Brahman, the Supreme Consciousness.

Brinjal: Aubergine/egg plant.

Chakali: Savoury, deep fried snack made with either whole-wheat flour, or a mixture of different flours and spices.

Chakali Maker: Mould of stainless steel or aluminium, with different shaped holes at the base, through which dough is pressed and then deep-fried to make *chakalis*.

Chakra: Sanskrit for 'wheel'. As many as nine different meanings. Here refers to one of the seven energy centres of the body.

Chapati: Common bread of India. Unleavened bread made with whole-wheat flour, toasted on a griddle and then puffed up over an open flame. Similar to a tortilla.

Chhinaal, also *Raand* (Marathi, Hindi), *Putain* (French): Whore.

Chhodo: Forget it; let it be.

Chidanandarupah: 'In the form of eternal bliss'.

Dada: See *Bhai*.

Dand: Push-up that ends with an arched back.

Darwaan: Door-keeper, or gate-keeper.

Dhabbu: Slang for a big marble made of stone; as opposed to glass marbles.

Dhak/Dhaak: Botanically, '*Butea monosperma*'. Also known as the 'Flame of the Forest.' Tree with bright orange flowers.

Dharma: Literally, 'way of life' or 'what one is genetically wired to be'. The four aims of human life are *dharma* (following your destined path), *artha* (creating wealth), *kama* (seeking pleasure), *moksha* (seeking liberation). Refer to *Grihasthashram* below.

Dhoti: Length of cloth worn by men, either as a simple sarong, or tied according to the style of the region.

Dhurrie: Rug.

Didi; also *Tai* (Marathi): Elder sister.

Ganapati, also *Ganesh*: Elephant-headed god, son of Lord Shiva and his consort Parvati.

Ganda: Red thread tied on wrist, signifying belonging between music teacher and student.

Ganesh: See *Ganapati*.

Ganesh Chaturthi: Festival celebrating the elephant headed god, Ganesh. Became a social festival legitimately used to spread concepts of independence from British colonialism.

Gharana: Of, or pertaining to a particular family, and its association with an art form. In this instance, of the Indore Gharana, the school of Indian classical music that is taught by the descendants or students of the Indore family.

Ghats: Mountain range on the west coast of India.

Gorakhchinch: Botanically, '*Adansonia digitata*' or the Indian baobab.

Grihasthashram: Family life; Second of the Four Stages

that a human being is supposed to pass through, during a lifetime. *Brahmacharyashram* is Stage of Celibacy (focus on gathering knowledge); *Grihasthashram* is Stage of Family Life (focus on creating wealth for family and society); *Vanaprashthrasham* is Stage of Withdrawal from Social Life (focus on knowledge and liberation); *Sanyashram* is Retreating from all Human Contact (focus on liberation). At each stage, the pursuit of the four different aims changes (See *Dharma* above).

Gulmohar: Botanically, '*Delonix regia*', a tree with orange or red flowers.

Guru: Teacher, master.

Gurubandhu: Brother, by virtue of having the same Guru.

Haan: 'Isn't it?', or 'Yes?'.

Haveli: Feudal mansion.

Hijda: Eunuch.

Idlis: Rice cakes.

Izzat: Honour.

Ji (See *Guru*ji, *Sardar*ji, *Pandit*ji): Respectful qualifier for one who is senior, or learned.

Jowar: Botanically, '*Sorghum vulgare*'. One of the sorghums grown on the plateau in Maharashtra. The coast (Konkan) grows mainly rice.

Jyotirling: Literally, 'Shiva as light'. *Jyoti* is light, *ling* is a stone in the shape of a penis, a metaphor for Shiva, the male principle; as opposed to Shakti, the female principle. Their union created the world.

Kaai: Literally, 'What?'.

Kadaklakshmi: Literally, 'The Severe Goddess'. In folk terms '*Jari Mai*', one who suffers for villagers who do not have access to any other way of redemption.

Kadamba: Botanically, '*Anthocephalus sinensis*'. A tree associated with Lord Krishna; with scented golf-ball sized flowers.

Karanji: A sweet prepared mainly during Diwali, the Festival of Lights, the biggest festival for North and West India. Boat-shaped, hard or soft flour outer with sweet stuffing within.

Kausalya suprajaa: Literally, 'the good son of Kausalya' a reference to Lord Ram, one of the incarnations of Lord Vishnu. The first phrase of one of the most commonly sung prayers.

Kharvas: Dish made out of colostrum of cows.

Kirlian photograph: 'Kirlian' refers to a photographic process that captures the auras/electromagnetic fields of the object of the picture.

Kokam: Botanically, '*Garcinia indica*'. The dried skin of its fruit is used as a sour spice, usually in curries along the Konkan coast.

Konkan: Indian name for Western coast of India stretching from Dahanu in Maharashtra to Kerala.

Kumkum: Vermillion, used by women in the parting of the hair, as a one of the signs of being married. Also used during *pujas*, on the forehead, or to make *bindis*.

Kurta: Loose, long shirt that is usually worn with a *pyjama* or a *dhoti*.

Laddoo: Generic term for small sweets made from flour, and rolled into balls.

Langot: Traditional Indian underwear, a single piece of

cloth tied around the groin.

Maadarchod: Literally, 'Mother-fucker'.

Maamaa: Mother's brother.

Maavshi: Mother's sister.

Mahabhutaas: see panchmahabhutaas

Mandap: Large tent or pavilion.

Mangalagaur: A festival celebrated on the Tuesdays (*'mangal' day*) of the rainy season. Five newlywed girls and five unwed girls stay awake till midnight by playing games to pray to Goddess Gauri, praying that they may have the same husband life after life.

Mangalsutra: Literally 'sacred, auspicious thread'; the symbol of marriage for most Indian women. Tied around her neck by the husband during the marriage ceremony, it consists of a pendant typically worn on a chain of black and gold beads. The pendant and chain may vary, depending on the caste/family into which the woman marries. Not to be taken off till the woman becomes a widow.

Mantra: Credo, chant.

Medu Vada: Flattish doughnut made with a mixture of lentils and rice.

Memsaahib: Wife of the *sahib*, the master.

Modak: Festival sweet, conical with fluted edges, created with different stuffings.

Mri: Root syllable, meaning 'measurement'.

Mriga: One of the twenty-eight constellations. When the moon is in *mriga* constellation on a particular day, heavy rains are expected.

Munja: A form of ghost; prayed to as god in some parts of Konkan.

Na: In this context, 'Isn't it?' or 'Right?'.

Namaskar, also *Namaste*: Literally 'I salute you': respectful form of greeting another.

Namaste: See *Namaskar*.

Neem: Botanically, '*Azadirachta indica*'. Its twigs are used as a toothbrush, its fruit is sour; used in cooking where kokam (see above) is not available.

Nirmaalya: Term for collection of flowers, garlands, sandalwood, water etc that had been offered to an idol and have now gone stale.

Nirvikalpasamaadhi: *Samadhi* is considered the fourth state of consciousness. *Nirvikalpasamaadhi* is the stage of *Samadhi* where the distinction between body, mind and soul vanish, and the person experiences oneness with the primordial energy.

Paarijaat: Botanically, '*Nyctanthus arbortristis*'. Also called the 'Tree of Sorrow' owing to the drooping foliage and flowers.

Padmashri: One of the highest civilian honours in India, given to people who are outstanding in their fields.

Pallu: Worn over the shoulder, the free end of a sari, the six or nine yard cloth that Indian women drape around themselves.

Panchmahabhutaas, also mahabhutaas : The five great elements: Earth, Water, Fire, Air and Space. They form the basis of material creation, starting with Space, which is closest to the pure consciousness (the source of all creation) and ending with Earth, the most solidified form of consciousness.

Papad: A fried accompaniment to most Indian meals, a flat mixture of ground lentils and rice, or *sago*, it is dried in the sun and stored for later use.

Parkar Polka: Petticoat and blouse.

Peda: Flattened sweet made with milk solids or chickpea flour, typical of certain states in Central and South India.

Peepal: Botanically, 'Ficus religiosa'. One of the five sacred trees in India. The Buddha attained enlightenment under a *peepal* tree. Hence venerated by both Hindus and Buddhists.

Pranaam: Literally 'Salutations', or 'I bow at your feet'. Used to acknowledge and seek blessings of an elder.

Puja: Ritualistic prayer, complete with offerings of food, flowers and drink to the gods.

Puraans: Ancient writings on mythology, for lay readers as opposed to scholars. Eighteen in number, mainly in verse, varying between 10,000 to 81,000 couplets.

Puran poli: A sweet preparation made predominantly with chickpea flour and cardomoms, layered like a pastry, rolled out and cooked like a *chapati*. Eaten either as is, or with warm milk.

Putain: See *Chhinaal*.

Pyjama: Type of pant worn with a loose shirt, or *kurta*.

Raag: A melodic 'concept'. While technically speaking each *raag* is simply a predetermined cluster of notes, it is left to the musician to expound its 'concept'.

Raand: See *Chhinaal*.

Riyaaz: Daily practice, especially towards the achievement of a goal; in this case towards the attainment of knowledge in the field of music.

Saadhu: Ascetic; hermit; holy man.

Saala: Literally, 'brother-in-law'. Slang connotation is 'I fucked your sister'.

Saali: Female version of 'saala'.

Sadhana: Devotion to a cause; dedication; practice.

Sahajasan: Literally, 'easy pose'. One of the many relaxing cross-legged poses in yogic exercises.

Saheb: Master.

Sammelan: Festival.

Samzhi: 'Understood; understand?'.

Sant: Saint.

Shaagird: Pupil.

Shaligraam: A black stone, the size of an acorn, worshipped as a symbol of Lord Vishnu.

Shataavadhaani: Capable of being simultaneously aware of a hundred events.

Sherwani: Two or three piece outfit worn by men, rather like a *pyjama* and *kurta*, except that the influence is distinctly Mughal, and may also include a stole to be worn around the arms, or across the shoulders.

Shishya: Disciple.

Shivoham: 'I am Shiva'.

Shloka: Verse, part of a prayer.

Smashaan: Cremation ground.

Sona: Literally, gold. Here, used as 'my precious one'.

Subbulakshmi: One of the greatest exponents of carnatic (South Indian, as opposed to Hindustani, which is North Indian) style of music; known especially for devotional songs.

Taalim: Practice.

Tai: See *Didi*.

Taluka: District, as opposed to village.

Tayyari: Preparation, readiness.

Thumri: A semiclassical song; usually about a girl's love for Lord Krishna.

Topi: Cap.

Tulasi: Botanically, '*Ocimum sativum*'. It represents Goddess Vrinda, and hence worshipped along with Lord Vishnu. A permanent fixture in the courtyards of most Indian homes.

Tussore: A form of strong, coarse brown silk.

UP: Uttar Pradesh, a state in North India.

Vilambit: The slow section of the performance of a *raag*; the faster section is called *drut*.

Zari: Silver or gold thread woven into cloth, either as a border, or in motifs throughout the weave.

Phrases

Chup re saala: 'Shut up, you *saala* (see '*saala*' above)!'

Deva re deva: 'Oh my God'; 'Dear Lord!'

Mhaataara re mhaatara: 'Old man...hey old man!'

Sadaa sukhi raho: Literally 'Always be happy' – a blessing bestowed by an elder.

Theek hai: 'It's okay' 'So be it.'

Yere, yere paavsaa, tula deto paisa: A ditty in Marathi. It offers a bribe to the rain.